The Flame of Heaven

By

Andrew P. Wright

Eloquent Books
New York, New York

Copyright 2008
All rights reserved - Andrew P. Wright

No part of this book may be reproduced or transmitted in any form or by any means, graphic, electronic, or mechanical, including photocopying, recording, taping, or by any information storage retrieval system, without the permission, in writing, from the publisher.

Eloquent Books
An imprint of AEG Publishing Group
845 Third Avenue, 6th Floor - 6016
New York, NY 10022
www.eloquentbooks.com

ISBN: 978-1-60693-144-8
SKU: 1-60693-144-X

Printed in the United States of America

Book Design: Roger Hayes

Dedication

To Kathryn and the boys with love.

And to Noel and John, men who value the truth.

Andrew P. Wright

Prologue

Elijah has returned! The effeminate and all too audible whisper ran through the gaggle of eunuchs gathered on the fifth stair of the throne room and broke over the prophets of Baal, many of whom looked on in wonder at this wild man from the desert as he walked boldly toward the throne. Elijah stood on the third broad stair from the throne and struck his staff upon the marble floor opposite the prophets.

This dirty and disheveled old man dressed in the hide of a stinking camel, with his wild hair and unoiled beard, could it truly be he who commanded the weather, the very domain of Baal the great? It was said that this prophet of the Lord, who leaned on his staff like a geriatric, prayed to the God of Heaven, and that this God heard Elijah and had stolen the weather scepter from Baal's hand and had brought a great drought to the land. No rain had fallen in Israel for three years while he, Elijah, had not the courage to face the prophetess of Baal, Queen Jezebel, but had bolted like a hare down its hole, into the far reaches of the desert, escaping the persecutions of Jezebel's priests. And now, the prophets of Baal reminded each other in sly whispers, this same Elijah had returned; and it was at just the right moment too. Jezebel was away, visiting with her family in Sidonia. What audacity: as if his curse were not enough, he had summoned the king.

The kohl black around King Ahab's eyes and his well-oiled hair and handsome face could not hide the lines of rage etched into his brow. When he saw the prophet, a snarl of hate set on his face. His eyes scanned the restless sea of whispering bodies. No one dared meet his gaze. An uneasy quiet settled upon the throne room. Between the great pillars, only the echo of rustling cloth and the soft patter of the eunuch's sandaled feet on the marbled floor could be heard, as they elbowed each other to be nearer the action. "Is it you, you troubler of Israel?" Ahab spoke these words quietly, surprising even himself because of the fierce hatred that threatened to overwhelm his heart.

The prophet's steady brown eyes regarded the king. If there was fear in his old heart it did not show, not even as the captain of the guard drew closer to him.

The jangle of the captain's armor had sent more imposing men than Elijah to their knees. The armed man towered over the prophet.

"On your knees!" he shouted and, gripping Elijah's tunic, he tried to force the old man into submission.

All were amazed to see the great muscles of the captain's shoulders bunch with his effort to force the old man down, but he could not. The captain and the old man appeared to be dancing together. A light wave of laughter broke over the unseemly spectacle.

King Ahab raised his hand, and the captain, flushed with embarrassment, withdrew with a bow.

Elijah flashed a grin at the observers. "I have not troubled Israel; but you have, and your father's house, because you have forsaken the commandments of the Lord and followed Baal," he said easily, his voice loud enough to carry across the whole throne room.

A hiss of resentment rose from the gathered throng. The captain of the guard lunged forward again and struck the prophet on the mouth. The old man staggered under the blow, but did not fall.

Another ripple of laughter washed through the audience of eunuchs and officials. Obrahim, the chief priest of Baal, tall and strong as a date palm, with his black coils of oiled hair in the Babylonian style, stood at the king's side. He bent and whispered in the king's ear. The king nodded. A wicked smile split Obrahim's blade-like face.

Again the king lifted his hand, "You are bold, old man, to come before me and slander the god of Jezebel, your queen."

At the name of the queen, Elijah's head snapped up and his eyes moved steadily over the faces of the approximately forty people present in the throne room.

Had the great prophet shown a sign of fear at the name of Jezebel? Could it be that he feared Jezebel more than Ahab? This incensed the king even further.

Instead of fear, the king then heard rich laughter break from the prophet's throat. The prophet wiped the blood from his lips.

"Is the great King Ahab so frightened of an old man that he must have his captain before him and his chief priest whispering lies of the black arts into his ears?"

The Lord's prophet laughed even harder and his eyes were merry.

Ahab watched Elijah carefully—*perhaps he had only imagined the prophet's fear a moment ago. It was a pity Jezebel was away visiting her family in Sidonia. She had a way with men. It would have been an interesting contest to watch.*

Elijah raised his hand this time and spoke, "Come, let us see how great you are and how great your gods are! Have all of Israel assemble before you at Mount Carmel with all four hundred and fifty prophets of Baal and the four hundred prophets of Asherah, who serve Jezebel and who murdered the prophets of the Lord! Let us have a contest. Let us see whose God is greater, the Lord the God of Heaven, or Baal the God of Thunder!"

Obrahim's face lit again. He leaned over and whispered into the king's ear, "Surely this man is a fool, my King. Baal is strong and will defeat this wild camel of the desert."

The king regarded the wizened face before him. *Obrahim was right, of course. Why not show Israel once and for all that their god was no match for Baal? Yet the heart of the king quailed within him. Why?*

The Flame of Heaven

"Let it be as you have said!" King Ahab shouted with a knowing smile playing about his lips.

"We will have a contest. You and your god against the prophets of Baal and their god. Send for all the men of Israel to gather and to stand before Mount Carmel!"

☙❧ ☙❧ ☙❧

At Mount Carmel, Elijah stood before the assembled host, alone and small. He raised his voice. "I am the only prophet of the Lord, but Baal's prophets number four hundred and fifty! Let two bulls be brought and cut into pieces and put the pieces on wood. Then you call on the name of your god, and I will call on mine! The god who answers by the flame of heaven; he is indeed God!"

So the prophets of Baal prepared their sacrifice. Obrahim, their chief priest, turned with a sneer on his face.

"Will you not flee again, Elijah?"

Elijah remained silent and watched as their ceremony began. They called with loud voices upon the Baal to manifest himself, but to no avail; soon they brought a frightened young priest forward and bent him over the altar.

"No, please no, no!" he screamed, his young face contorted in fear.

"The god must feed!" Obrahim said and lifted up the young priest's head by the forelock, exposing his neck. He cut deep into the exposed throat with a look of lust etched upon his narrow face. The blood gushed from the young priest's neck across the altar. Obrahim cut deeper still until the whole head came off in his hands. He lifted the head to the heavens and screamed the name of Baal.

Elijah looked away in disgust. He started to prepare his own sacrifice.

Obrahim's act of cruelty seemed to unlock the gates of inhibition in the watching prophets of Baal. They began to openly blaspheme the Lord of Heaven and cut themselves with their curved knives. They raved on all morning, but even then there was no response from the heavens.

As this spectacle continued, Elijah built his altar, carefully selecting twelve stones according to the number of tribes of the sons of Jacob. He dug a deep trench around the altar and then put the wood and the pieces of meat on the altar. Next he said, so that all could hear and understand, "Pour twelve jars of water onto the offering."

A murmur ran through the crowding throng of people. They were amazed at Elijah's calm assurance in the face of the fierce blasphemies and taunts of the prophets. As the water ran from the altar and filled the deep trench, Elijah glanced up and saw King Ahab lean over to one of his advisers with a worried expression on his face.

At about midday, in the time of the offering of oblation, Elijah cried in a loud voice so that all could hear:

"Enough, you whores!" He turned to the altar and raised his arms and said in a strong and steady voice, "O, Lord of Heaven, let it be known this day that you are God, that I am your servant, and that I have done all these things at your bidding! Answer me, Lord, so that the people may know you!"

There was complete silence as Elijah called upon the Lord a second time. Elijah cried out a third time.

A single voice broke into laughter. King Ahab rose from his throne. "Where is your God now, Elijah!" he roared.

The people looked up at their king and then across at Elijah. A wicked smile played across the face of Obrahim, who stood to one side, his head bent in a gesture of sardonic amusement.

Suddenly a bright golden light suffused the mountaintop. Ahab's head jerked up, his eyes wide. Within several heartbeats the golden glow turned into the color of burned copper, almost too bright to look at.

The king cried out and reeled backwards holding his eyes. Elijah himself fell to his knees. The whole throng of people ducked for cover. A tumult of cursing and shoving broke out among the frightened crowd of onlookers, but there was nowhere to hide. Great dread pressed down on them in that place as they looked up into the boiling sky. There followed a

The Flame of Heaven

mighty wall of sound, as if a million angry voices roared their fury, and then, from the Eternal Throne, there fell the flames of Heaven!

Chapter 1

Dr. Thomas Dekker's clear gray eyes took in the majestic Ionic columns that supported the facade of the British Museum. He adjusted the collar of his dark coat against the chilling wind that whipped down Great Russell Street. His brisk long stride and cheerful ruddy face spoke eloquently of the excitement threatening to burst from him. The breath bellowed from his large six-foot-three frame as he took the steps two at a time and entered the museum's magnificent portico. Although he had been to this museum a hundred times or more, it still gave him a thrill; such treasures it possessed.

The phone call had come last night, and he and his young wife had danced around the small lounge room of their Bloomingdale flat.

"They want to offer me the job, the job, the job!" Dekker had sung, as he led Kate in a fairly poor imitation of a waltz. Kate grinned up at her husband.

"Don't get ahead of yourself, Dekker. It's the second interview, and it's important, but there are still bound to be other candidates."

"Oh ye of little faith," Dekker said and then grinned boyishly. "Besides, how many other people can interpret ancient Babylonian fluently? Come on Katie, how many do you know? I'll bet you there's a whole bushel of Babylonians in the flat next door."

Kate had pushed him away gently and looked up into his eyes and then up at his slightly wild, straw-colored hair. "I don't doubt you . . . and we're going to have to put some powerful gel or something on that hair of yours. We want you looking respectable."

Dekker looked into Kate's smiling blue eyes and ran his hand through her long chestnut hair, "I declare myself the luckiest man alive!"

☙ ☙ ☙

Now, inside the museum, he took the stairs to the second floor, this time more slowly; he didn't want to be out of breath and flushed at the interview—that would not do. The administration desk swam into view. He adjusted his striped tie nervously. All set.

Dekker was quickly ushered into a thickly carpeted, rectangular room by the young, rather pretty redheaded receptionist. Three people, two men and a woman, sat on a very modern and imposing semicircular lounge chair in the middle of the room, their backs toward him.

The room faced a large rectangular window, which looked on to the huge, open atrium in the middle of the Museum. An iridescent light shone through the massive skylight in the atrium and spilled through their window, filling the room with a soft pearly glow. Besides this light, a soft luminescence fell from oyster lamp fittings in the ceiling that strategically lit the black marble bust of a Pharaoh and the statue of an Assyrian gryphon. A large bookshelf full of leather-bound books filled the far wall.

The trio was in low conversation. He wondered vaguely why the receptionist had not let the trio know he had entered the room. Because of this oversight, he was uncomfortably aware they had not registered his presence.

" . . . not likely to recover," he heard the woman say. "I spoke with Dr. Sikes on the phone this morning. He says the professor is speaking almost exclusively in a Mesopotamian dialect, with one or two lucid moments in English and those moments are . . . well, frightening. Something about a curse. It appears to be a complete mental breakdown . . ."

The receptionist at his side coughed delicately. Dekker noticed the seated woman start; the other two grew still, like men do when they have been surprised, heads bent forward.

An awkward silence filled the room as Dekker was led around the lounge upon which they sat to a lone chair on the other side of a broad, shiny-surfaced coffee table. None of them got up, and it would have been impossible to shake hands with any of them across the considerable breadth of the table.

"Good God, Kirsten! Honestly, were you not taught any manners," spat the woman.

This is not going too well, thought Dekker. He could feel his face getting hot.

"Sorry, Madam," said the receptionist called Kirsten. "It's just I did not want to interrupt you."

Dekker glanced at Kirsten; she did not appear flustered or in the least bit sorry, but rather cool. The slight Scottish lilt to her accent added to the sense of defiance, thought Dekker; he struggled to suppress a grin. Kirsten's large brown eyes held the eye of the older woman steadily.

The woman flicked her finger, indicating Kirsten should go.

"And close the door behind you!" she added sharply.

Dekker's surprise grew. He recognized one of the trio immediately. Lord Ashworth, his back ramrod straight, sat in the center of the group. He was a man Dekker associated with important international affairs in Britain; something to do with the UN. Dekker had very little interest in politics but recalled several half-watched news events on TV recently where this man had featured prominently; he always seemed to be involved in committee hearings in Europe and the International Court.

Dekker stood with a half smile on his face and waited to be invited to sit. The three people looked up at him from where they sat, their collective expression expectant and watchful. A look of bemused embarrassment suffused Dekker's gray eyes as the awkward silence continued.

"Ahh, I'm sorry. Have I come at a bad time?" Dekker asked evenly.

The man he recognized as Lord Ashworth smiled. The smile did not reach his hooded eyes. Dekker noted the almost girlish redness of his lips as they smeared across his perfect teeth. He was taller than his companions, his balding head glossy in the pearly light. What remained of his dark hair was close cropped.

"Please . . ." Lord Ashworth said, indicating with a languid movement of his hand that Dekker should sit.

That one syllable carried with it all the rounded Oxford breeding and sense of command Dekker recognized immediately. He did not fail to notice the studied slight as Lord Ashworth continued to sit.

Dekker sat down obediently. The other two also remained seated, statue-like in their stillness—the expression on their faces watchful.

The woman was painfully thin with stiff, elaborately coiffured platinum blonde hair and bright blue, but somehow extinguished, eyes. The other gentleman, swarthy and thickset with shoulders bulging under his tight-fitting jacket, stared at Dekker with coal black eyes. He looked Arabic.

Another awkward silence built. Dekker forced a smile, but a stubborn feeling of annoyance grew inside him. He sensed that they were enjoying his discomfort.

Game playing thought Dekker—he stared back at the shiny head of Lord Ashworth.

The woman spoke suddenly.

"Doctor, ah . . . Dekker is it?"

Dekker raised his eyebrows, curling the left corner of his mouth and nodding his head slightly. The woman frowned.

"Dr. Dekker," her voice cracked again, brittle dry. It matched her body perfectly.

"Please, just 'Dekker' will do," he answered breezily. He sensed that she was somewhat taken aback, and childishly he admitted to himself he enjoyed that feeling.

"Mr. Dekker . . . I'm sure you will recognize Lord Ashworth, one of the most important patrons of this museum and European adviser to the United Nations and the chief prosecutor at the International Court."

"I do," Dekker said. Lord Ashworth smiled a thin smile.

"I am Sibyl Hardacre, curator of the museum and this is Mr. Dupree, Lord Ashworth's ah . . . bodyguard."

"Pleasure to meet you," he lied and smiled again. The tiniest of alarm bells started to ring inside his mind. *A rather illustrious panel for a somewhat innocuous position within a museum,* he thought to himself.

"A Mr. Simons conducted my first interview. I see he is not with us today?" Dekker added.

Sibyl Hardacre sat silent for a moment with her mouth slightly open. A half laugh escaped her as she watched Dekker.

"I see, Mr. Dekker, that you are a man of acute observation and it would appear a man not easily intimidated . . . that is good. You see this ah . . . position we have available is a rather sensitive one, and so Mr. Simons' services have been dispensed with. The right candidate will not only be a man of impeccable academic credentials, Mr. Dekker, and we know you possess those, but also a man with a great deal of discretion . . . and trustworthiness. One could almost say a real patriot."

Dekker sat silent for several heartbeats. The three sets of eyes bore into him.

No, they were not joking, obviously.

"Well, Ms. Hardacre, Lord Ashworth, you are quite right. I'm not intimidated. I'm not sure that my courage . . ." Dekker could see from their expressions that he had taken the wrong tack. He started again: "I believe myself to be a trustworthy man and my cred . . ."

"Dekker!" Lord Ashworth interrupted. "Dekker?" said Lord Ashworth again as if speaking to a small child. He smiled his pasty smile.

"We have perhaps not been entirely fair with you. You are the preferred candidate." Several seconds of silence followed.

Dekker wasn't sure how he felt, at once elated and surprised, but somehow rather wary

"Dekker, relax young man. We have had to take precautions. I know you will understand once you see what we have before us. The position entails a high degree of secrecy."

"I'm . . . sorry. I don't understand?" Dekker said slowly. "Your advertisement spoke about the position of coordinator for the Mesopotamian and Babylonian collection, an academic philologist who is able to interpret cuneiform and understand Babylonian and Sumerian."

Dekker noticed a light buzzing sound. Dupree took a pager from his belt and looked at its screen, then leaned over and whispered into Lord Ashworth's ear.

Lord Ashworth gave a prim nod.

"Dekker!" he said again. "Come. We know your credentials and your record . . . impeccable, very impressive. What we have had to make sure of is something altogether different. Forget the collection for now. We have something far more exciting!" The pasty smile again. "Something, you could say, of . . . well, international importance."

Dekker felt his discomfort grow, but said nothing. He smiled.

What was Ashworth talking about?

"You've had to make sure of something?" Dekker asked in a mystified tone, still trying to be polite. "Forgive my impertinence, but just exactly what is this something you are referring to?"

This time there was no pasty smile from Lord Ashworth.

"We have something in our possession of the utmost importance, and we need your help, Dekker."

Dekker scanned the trio again. Sibyl sat quietly. Dupree, stolid and taciturn, regarded him without expression. Despite his misgivings he was intrigued.

"You are familiar with Professor Whitely's work, are you not, Doctor?"

Dekker's eyebrows rose in surprise. He had studied ancient civilizations under Professor Whitely at Cambridge and knew that Whitely worked closely with the museum.

"I see you are. Yes, Professor Whitely was working for us, for his country, on this project, but has unfortunately taken a turn for the worse."

Ashworth regarded Dekker through his hooded eyes once again. Dekker was starting to find that particular expression of Ashworth's annoying.

"I think you may have overheard some of our conversation when you were . . . ah ushered in unexpectedly."

"Well, I must apologize, but . . ."

Lord Ashworth held up his hand to silence Dekker. "Dupree?"

The bodyguard withdrew a sheet of paper and pushed it over the coffee table toward Dekker.

Dekker looked down at it, not moving. His heart thumping, he read the first line.

> Top Secret
> By order of Her Majesty's Government

"A secrecy declaration?" he said. "So, I take it I've won the job then."

All three burst into laughter. Dekker flushed visibly.

"My goodness, Dekker, you are slow. Sign the form. In a sense, it is too late to withdraw now. Your country needs your skills urgently, and . . . well, you have already overheard your first top secret conversation."

No smile this time.

Dekker felt his adrenaline rise. He heartily resented Lord Ashworth's bullying manner. Frankly, the appeal to serve his country was just too much.

"Look, I'd rather not. I really must know what it is I'm getting into before I sign anything."

A smile twitched Ashworth's lips.

"Ah yes, that's all very grown up, Dekker. We haven't spoken about money yet. Let's do that. Tell me, how much do you earn now?"

Dekker swallowed hard. They were living off Katie's salary at the moment. He could feel himself flush again.

"I understand, young Dekker. We all need to start somewhere, but really your skills, while impressive and so on—well! They are rather specialized?"

A wave of resentment broke in Dekker's heart, but he could feel it was a sullen, compromising little wave. Still, he had his pride—this was too much.

"Lord Ashworth, Ms Hardacre, Mr. Dupree, I thank you for your time, but I'm afraid I cannot agree to something I know nothing of."

At this, he stood.

Dekker was taken aback by the sheer fury that blazed from Lord Ashworth's eyes.

"Is that your final decision then, young man?" Ashworth snapped.

Dekker stood awkwardly, not quite knowing what to do, his hopes dashed.

"Well, sir. If you would let me know what . . ."

Ashworth laughed again, the sound very brittle.

"Oh, I see, my apologies, this has been a great misunderstanding. Signing the document doesn't mean you get the job. What I mean is you can still back out of it if you really want to. It just means we have a legal, well, position to work from should you inadvertently speak about this to anyone—and we do mean anyone, Dekker. Sit down, Dekker, sit, sit!"

A great sense of relief flooded over Dekker, but the small warning voice would not be quiet, his heart still pounding.

"Oh, I do beg your pardon. I was under the impression you had said . . ."

"Under the impression, hey? You hear that Sibyl? No, impressions are no good. This is serious business."

Sibyl rasped her laughter again.

Dupree opened his suit jacket and took a pen from the inside pocket. As he did so, Dekker noted the pistol butt suspended from a shoulder holster. Dupree handed Dekker the pen, then pushed the paper across the coffee table.

Dekker hesitated—the warning voice had become a shout ringing out loudly in his head. He pushed aside the feeling.

Was he not his own man? Isn't this what men did; make hard decisions? Besides he was sick and tired of not having a job.

The image of Katie's blue eyes swam into his inner vision.

"Well, sign up. I cannot explain anything until you have signed the secrecy declaration," said Lord Ashworth quietly.

Ashworth's effeminate mouth was now more like a snarl, his eyes without expression. Sibyl's eyes, Dupree's eyes, all deadpan, were not giving much away.

Dekker swallowed hard. He signed the paper with what he hoped looked like a professional flourish. He felt weak, compromised and thoroughly out of his depth.

He managed a wan smile. "So, I'm all ears," he said as coolly as possible.

Lord Ashworth looked down, for a moment. "I'd like to invite you and your wife, Katie, is it? Ah yes . . . to my place in the country. Just west of here, not far from Salisbury actually."

Dekker was taken aback. *How did Ashworth know Katie's name.* He felt sick, but did not voice his apprehension—*he must have mentioned Katie's name in the last interview.*

"Well, I'll have to consult my wife and yes it is Katie. I really must be more careful about what information I put on my resume in future." Dekker smiled.

He viewed their bemused expressions with satisfaction. Lord Ashworth stared at him for a moment with his hooded-eye expression. Dekker could see he was struggling to keep his temper in check.

"I know you to be a reasonable man, Dekker. I would not have bothered with you otherwise. This is a highly sensitive . . ." Ashworth began.

"So you keep on saying, Lord Ashworth. But if you prize my reason so much, why is it that you won't tell me what it is you would have me do."

Lord Ashworth smiled, this time pleasantly.

"Ah, that is what we will be paying for. A man who knows his own mind . . . good. No, Dekker, I don't want to tell you. I want to show you. I don't want to prejudice you in any way you see. I will show you and then you can make up your mind."

Dekker looked at Ashworth for two heartbeats.

"Well, okay, what's the address?" He glanced at his watch. "It's midday now. I'll talk to Katie and we'll meet you there at, say, five?"

"No need. We can leave now. Katie is already on her way."

"What!" Dekker said, his heart pounding again.

Lord Ashworth stood. "Dekker, if you are to work for me, you must not question my authority. You really are being tiresome. We could not have your wife left behind."

"Yes, but how did you know I'd agree to, to any of this!"

"Good God, Dekker, there you go again! You're very slow for someone who has such intelligence. Let me spell this out for you. You are now working for Her Majesty's government, whether you like it or not. Because you are now exposed to a great power, you and your wife will be in considerable danger. We have taken the liberty of making sure your wife is safe. I presume the safety of your wife means something to you?"

Dekker simply stared, too surprised to speak.

"That message Dupree received was to tell us that your wife is now safe and sound with us."

A great rage entered Dekker. He felt so incensed at the effrontery of this man that he could hardly speak.

Sibyl and Lord Ashworth looked at each other and smiled wryly.

"Dupree," said Lord Ashworth. "Show the young doctor your badge please."

Obediently, Dupree flipped open the jacket he wore to reveal his police badge.

"Have you heard of the Civil Cooperation Bureau? No? Not many people have: a new secret service. We live in dangerous times, Dekker."

The fight went out of Dekker then. Ashworth smiled his pasty smile.

"Come now, Dekker. None of this would be necessary if you would only cooperate. Your country needs your help and that very urgently. I have, we have all tried to be civil. After all, we are the good guys—and I know you will want to help when you understand more fully that for which we need you."

Chapter 2

Dekker was ushered out of the back doors of the British Museum, past a gaggle of squabbling girls in their school uniforms and several groups of enthusiastic tourists. The only person who did seem to catch his eye was Kirsten, the receptionist, but she ducked her head behind her monitor as Sibyl sailed past, glaring down at her.

A fine looking gray Bentley and a black Mercedes-Benz awaited them on Russell Square, the back entrance to the museum, engines ticking.

"We'll meet you at the house," said Ashworth over his shoulder to Dupree.

"Yes, sir," said Dupree in his gravely voice. Ashworth and Sibyl were ushered into the Bentley. Dekker was ushered into the back seat of the Benz; Dupree followed.

Dekker felt like a prisoner. He noticed a very fit-looking male driver. Next to him, in the passenger seat, sat a middle-aged woman in police uniform. The driver revved the engine and they were whisked quickly into a stream of traffic, heading northwest.

"So, Dupree, do you care to explain how it is that Her Majesty's police force now has the power to spy on civilians?" Dekker said in his most acid tone.

Dupree did not answer.

"How about you? Got any answers?" Dekker said to the woman sitting in the passenger seat. "If you've forced my wife I'll . . ."

Andrew P. Wright

"Dekker," said the woman evenly, "watch your tongue. You're on the team now and that means there is a hierarchy of command. If you understood the gravity of the situation you find yourself in, you would cooperate immediately." The policewoman looked to her right and left dramatically.

"We're not out of the woods yet. Go as fast as you can," she said to the driver.

"Oh, please. I'm a doctor of philology you blistering dolt. Who would be interested in me? I have had it from Ashworth himself that you lot bugged my wife and me and that she is now in your custody." Dekker gave Dupree a quick glance to see if he would react to the lie.

The woman turned around in her seat. Her light blue eyes took him in coolly.

Dekker held her gaze. "And for your information, I am not on the team. I am still to make up my mind about that."

The woman grinned, then snorted derisively. "Is that what you think? Listen, Dekker. You academic types are all the same—fine on theory, but not much good in a real scrape. Well, this is the real thing, my boy. And by the way, your wife is safe and in our care for good reason. Just yesterday, MI6 notified the authorities that two so-called "allies" of ours had sent hit squads to our shores. If you knew what danger you were in just being associated with this project, you would be groveling your thanks. As for the bugging, we had to make sure you were the genuine article."

Next to him Dupree cleared his throat and shook his head. The woman glared at him.

Dekker swallowed hard. So, his suspicions had been confirmed. They had been bugged.

"Article? You know, people like you always have your excuses, don't they? Do you think anything can be justified as mere expedience because you have some cause or other? I did not volunteer for this position, you know!"

The woman in the passenger seat chuckled to herself and turned around to face the front again. "No Doctor Dekker, you did not 'volunteer'. You are a paid professional and very much on the team," she threw back over her shoulder. "Sit still and hold your tongue, and we'll soon have you reunited with wifey-pie. Dupree, you know what to do if he tries to do anything heroic."

"Yes, Sergeant," Dupree said. His dark piggy eyes lit up at the thought.

Dekker was so taken aback at this turn of events, he could not think of anything more to say. These people were the police after all.

Chapter 3

Kirsten parted the vertical blinds ever so slightly to the office window and looked down into Russell Square, opposite the museum's back entrance. Her other hand held back the length of her red hair as she leaned over. Her intelligent brown eyes took in the scene below. Lord Ashworth and Sibyl were whisked away to who-knows-where in their Bentley, and Dekker, poor Dekker, was obviously being forced to go with his entourage against his will. The Mercedes-Benz moved off with Dekker inside.

The young woman scanned the square frantically for her contacts—where were they? They were supposed to be waiting in the square. She carefully let the blind fall back into position and then hurried to her bag, found her cell phone, and made a call.

"Yes, it's me. Dekker has been taken in a black Benz, and Lord Ashworth and Miss Hardacre in a gray Bentley . . ." She paused for a second, listening. "You saw them? Where are you?"

She ran back to the blind, lifting it carefully. Two well-muscled young men sauntered across the square to a waiting, white-panel van; one held a mobile phone. If Dekker had been present he would have recognized two of the tourists he'd just passed in the atrium of the museum.

She smiled to herself—real cool customers, those two. One of them, Declan, shot a glance over his shoulder. He grinned up at her window as he got into the passenger seat of the van.

"As far as I can make out, heading west," she said into the phone. "They took the road to Piccadilly and I presume the A40. They're heading for Ashworth's estate, I gather." Kirsten turned and looked intently at the door.

"Dekker is obviously going against his will. I take it all went according to plan?" Lewis said.

"Yes, he overheard some of their conversation, but to be honest, I don't think that ploy of ours was entirely necessary. Lord Ashworth is such an ass he managed to put Dekker off all by himself," Kirsten said.

Lewis chuckled as he started the van. "Well done, anyway."

"I'd better go. The walls have ears around here. And thank you, Lewis." Kirsten smiled nervously and ended the call.

Chapter 4

The fire fell with a brilliant golden fury. Terrified, Obrahim was transfixed by the spectacle for several moments. He recovered quickly. He knew he was in trouble and how capricious the people of Israel were. His priests had been less than gentle with them these last three years. Now, no fear he could evoke would save him. He clambered to his feet, his frenzied eyes seeking a path of escape. There was no other way but into the desert. Jezebel would be able to persuade the king to protect him.

Obrahim scrambled through the prostrated, tumult of bodies, all still reeling from Heaven's fury. He held his curved knife out, ready to strike down anyone who tried to stop his escape.

He was at the edge of the crowd now—the slope of the mountain spilled him into a shallow wadi, which ran diagonally down the slope and out into the desert. He slipped behind some loose boulders. Looking back at the scene he saw Elijah scramble to his feet again.

"Men of Israel!" screamed the Prophet of God.

"How long will you blaspheme your God and countenance the presence of these perverts among you? Fall upon these false prophets and these evil priests!"

With that, Elijah threw back his cloak, revealing a sword. He surged into the cowering throng of Baal's prophets and laid the first of them into the dust with a powerful thrust.

Other men followed. Soon there was a great slaughter as the priests of Baal, screaming and pleading for mercy, tried to escape the anger of the people. They struck back with their curved knives and one or two of their opponents fell, but they were no match for the sword and the fury of Heaven. Obrahim looked on in terror. He flicked his eyes up to where the king stood. The king himself was in great fear and did not dare to try to stop the carnage below him. Obrahim crept on his belly among the stones of the wadi. When he was out of sight of the rampaging slaughter, he got up and ran as fast as he could. He headed north. If he were very fortunate, he would be able to find Jezebel's camel train on the road back from Baal Bek before they entered Israel and warn her about Elijah's return. Someone had betrayed them. Someone had told Elijah that Jezebel was away visiting her people, but whom? The prophet would never have faced her. She terrified men, even the great prophets of Israel. They had all run from her before. Soon they would again.

Chapter 5

Jezebel strode into the throne room with a pale-faced Obrahim in her train. The head eunuch had told the king of her arrival only that afternoon. The truth is the king had been in some trepidation all week at her return. She would not be happy at the loss of her priests, he knew that. She stood now before the seated king; her eyes blazed green fury.

"Flames of Heaven! Flames of Heaven! Is that all the excuse you have, O' King? You allowed my priests to be slaughtered! Only Obrahim escaped, and no thanks to you!" Jezebel screeched.

The king sat slumped upon his throne, a look of scornful amusement playing over his features. "My Queen . . . how wonderful to see you again. Are your people well?"

Jezebel's lips compressed into a flat line of poorly suppressed anger. "My priests!" she screamed.

The king raised his hand, nodding his head in sympathy. "You must understand. We Israelites believe in the God of Heaven. When he speaks, we are compelled to obey. If I had ordered Elijah to stop the slaughter, the people would have turned on me."

"Have you too then gone back to the God who cannot be seen? Where is he now?" Jezebel gesticulated wildly with her arms.

"Why does he not strike me down with fire? Bah! Men! You are all cowards!"

The Flame of Heaven

King Ahab stood, his face stony and eyes hard as agate. "Jezebel, you will watch your tongue before me!" he shouted and took a slow step toward her.

"There was nothing I could do. And if the people learn that Obrahim has escaped, they will want his head too."

The king looked down at Obrahim. The chief priest of Baal kneeled before the throne, his forehead touching the floor, not daring to look up—*he was a wily one. How had the man escaped?*

"In their present mood, I'm very inclined to give the people what they want," King Ahab added.

"You would not dare!" shouted Jezebel. The king noted the scribes and eunuchs moving restlessly in the shadows. Fear and pride surged together in his breast. Pride won out. He lunged toward the queen and caught her by the lower jaw, squeezing her face tightly between his powerful, gold-ringed fingers.

"My Queen, you will curb your tongue, or lose it!" he snarled.

Jezebel glared up at him, straining against his grip.

"As for Elijah, if you are so brave, you may seek him out and do as you please with him, but then you will face the people of Israel by yourself. I warn you that they do not take kindly to the murder of their prophets. I wash my hands of this event. If it is mentioned in my presence again, that person will die!"

He released Jezebel's smarting face and smiled down at her. "I will retire for the night. You look tired my Queen. Why do you not take some rest."

For all her courage Jezebel dared not defy the king again. It would mean instant death.

"As you say, my Lord. Leave this Prophet of Israel to me, and I will see to it that he troubles you no more."

Ahab looked a long time into Jezebel's fierce eyes.

"I warn you, my Queen, the Lord of Heaven lives. Even now, the hill upon which Elijah sacrificed still smolders with holy fire, and this after one week has passed. If you do not believe me, go and see for yourself the power of Heaven."

A long silence fell between them as they eyed each other.

King Ahab sighed, then added: "Be careful with Elijah; he is a man after God's own heart."

With these words, he turned abruptly and walked into the dark recesses of his chambers, dismissing the eunuchs and the scribe to whom he had been giving orders while seated on his throne.

The golden light of the oil lamps flickered in the nearly silent throne room; the only sounds were the tinkle of Jezebel's jewelry with each quick angry intake of her breath and the furtive slither of the eunuchs' sandals as they ducked for the cover of darkness in the vast hall.

The scribe sitting on his stool at the throne's foot carefully rolled the vellum scrolls. His styli made slight clicking sounds in the vast silence.

Jezebel's eyes flicked over the scribe and into the recesses of the hall.

Obrahim climbed laboriously from his knees. Jezebel's eyes flicked over him. They were crazed eyes, the eyes of the prophetess of Baal and not the queen. The voice that issued from Jezebel's lips was not hers either—low and cracked and dry as the desert rocks. "Eunuch! And you . . . scribe come here!"

The head eunuch came forward, trembling visibly, though it was a hot night.

"Tell the Prophet of the Lord that Jezebel seeks him," she whispered.

The eunuch bobbed his head and sped from the chamber, the fat of his body jouncing with each quick step.

Obrahim felt a sheer thrill of terror run through his body. He knew what was coming next.

"As for you, Obrahim, you will take me to the place of slaughter. I wish to look upon this 'fire-from-heaven'—oh, and bring the orb, the one that the Baal in the temple holds in his right hand."

Obrahim stared blankly at her. "My Queen . . ." he checked his sentence as he looked into the queen's eyes. The eyes of the Prophetess of Baal had pupils as small as pinpricks, the irises a dazzling green. Obrahim squirmed. He held her gaze for a few moments, then let his eyes fall. "Do you mean the orb in which we burn the incense?"

Jezebel stared at him stonily for a long moment.

"Bring your cloak with you, the crimson one for travel and then meet me at the stables. As soon as we have finished on the mountain, you will be going to Babylon."

"Yes my Queen," Obrahim said obsequiously and bowed deeply. Obrahim walked swiftly from the great hall, flicking a glance over to the scribe who waited quietly for the queen.

"What is your name scribe? I do not recognize you!"

"My name is Shelomo. I am the understudy of the chief scribe, Jahleel."

Jezebel's eyes flicked over his lithe frame.

"You look a little old to be an understudy. Where is Jahleel?"

The scribe bowed his head submissively.

"You say well my Queen. In fact I taught Jahleel. I was the chief scribe for the King's father. Now I am old and my services are used only when Jahleel is not available or when there is some need for obscure translation. To your second question my Queen, Jahleel has been taken ill."

Jezebel gazed at the scribe. His protocol and demeanor could not be faulted, but his answers were just a little too crisp. A warning flared in the back of Jezebel's mind, but she extinguished it irritably.

"How many languages do you read?"

"As many as are needful, your highness," said Shelomo fluently in the queen's Sidonian tongue.

The queen smiled mirthlessly.

"That is a proud answer Shelomo the scribe—and now I will test you. For my dictation you will need clay, not vellum. Put away the king's dispatches, they can wait. What I dictate to you is of far more import. I dictate to you in Babylonian, Old Phoenician and Persian."

Shelomo bowed again, his face a mask, "As you wish my Queen. They are three languages I know well."

Jezebel watched the deft movements of the scribe as he readied his tool. He readied the royal seal and wax and produced from a pouch the wedge-shaped Babylonian writing styli. Then he carefully but deftly unwrapped several moist clay tablets and looked up expectantly; they would dry quickly in the hot weather.

There was something about this quiet scribe, she thought. *There was no fear, his hands completely steady.*

Shelomo looked up expectantly with a slight smile on his lips. "Your majesty . . . the clay."

❦ ❦ ❦

The horseman approached the entrance to the cave carefully. He dismounted his horse quickly and tethered its reins to the nearest bush.

"Elijah, are you there?" he said in a loud whisper.

There was no answer. The man strode up the side of the wadi to the entrance of the cave. Coals smoldered balefully in a circle of stone. Thin clouds scudded across the full moon.

"Elijah!" the man called again, though not daring to shout.

A shadow detached itself from the far wall.

"Shelomo?" Elijah bowed to show his respect.

"My brother! You gave me a start. You are safe, thank God!" Shelomo noticed that Elijah wore his sword.

"You are wise to wear your sword, Brother. Make haste and flee from here. Jezebel has returned. Obrahim survived the massacre and is with her. They plan their revenge on you even now. I saw her arrive this afternoon. Then I saw the two of them near the stables and Obrahim carrying a burner, together with a letter for the chief priest at Babylon. I have just written that for her. She is planning mischief. Obrahim even tonight makes his way to Babylon."

"What does the queen write to the false prophets of Babylon?" Elijah said with interest.

Shelomo told Elijah what had been dictated to him by the queen.

The prophet nodded in the wan light, and Shelomo thought he saw Elijah shudder.

"There are deep and troubling matters afoot. I will do as you suggest and go into the desert once more." Elijah said.

There was silence between the two men for a moment.

"Will you be missed if you leave for several weeks?" Elijah said.

"No, I have just taken the king's dictations and besides Jahleel is on the mend. His nose runs."

Elijah chuckled. "Jahleel has ever been susceptible to illness, but he is a good man. Only follow Obrahim to Babylon, Shelomo. They're up to no good."

Elijah made his way down to Shelomo and threw his arms around him. Shelomo noted that Elijah had been weeping.

"Why are you sorrowful, my Brother?" said Shelomo.

Elijah drew back and his cheeks glistened with tears in the high moonlight.

"The Lord has revealed that I will never see you again on this earth," he said.

Shelomo nodded solemnly.

"Go friend, make haste. I will hide myself away from Jezebel. Do not worry about me."

Shelomo smiled painfully and then kissed Elijah on the cheeks three times. He turned abruptly and made his way down the wadi silently to his waiting mount, his eyes filled with tears.

Chapter 6

Kate ran to Dekker and threw her arms around his neck. He could see she had been crying.

"You're trembling," he said softly into her ear.

"They said you'd been hurt, that you'd fallen down a flight of stairs and broken your leg. They offered to take me to the hospital to see you, but then they brought me here instead." She looked up into his clouded eyes, "Dekker, what's going on? They refuse to tell me anything."

Dekker looked around the sparsely furnished lounge room. Only Dupree was present, together with a worn looking Victorian chaise lounge and two cracked leather-bound wingback club chairs. The French windows were heavily draped, but parted just enough to reveal a copse of silver birch–covered hills to the east and a thicket of hazel wood—a melancholy scene in the late afternoon light.

Dupree stood about ten paces off, enough distance, Dekker judged, to give them some privacy, but close enough to stop any mischief.

"It's a set up, Kate. They're government people. They need someone who can speak Babylonian and translate cuneiform, and they have my old professor here under some sort of duress, which's all I know. Some kind of object or manuscript has got them all hot and sweaty. Heaven alone knows what this is all about."

He looked down into her trusting blue eyes. "I'm so sorry I've got us into this mess, honey. I . . . they bugged our flat, Kate!"

Kate smiled up at him, but Dekker could see she was scared.

"How could you have known? You don't need to apologize. I'm just glad you're okay." She sighed to suppress a sob.

"Katie . . . Kate, all will be well. I'll give them what they want, and then we'll go our way. I stupidly agreed to sign a secrecy declaration. So now I have to cooperate."

Katie looked into his eyes again.

"I mean, it's a piece of archaeology, for heavens sake! I'm sure this is all just a massive overreaction on Lord Ashworth's part."

"Secrecy declaration?" Kate said, a look of concern spreading across her face.

"Yeah, they convinced me it was necessary. Though to be perfectly honest I'm not sure it makes a shred of difference. It just sort of gives this abduction a veneer of lawfulness and respectability."

"What do they want, Dekker?" Kate whispered.

"I don't know. They'll make the next move, and I'll see what I can do from there. Kate, these are heavy people. That bloke over there is a policeman and armed. Don't try to do anything heroic, no matter what they do to me. They won't hesitate to use force."

"How right you are, Dekker," said a cool voice behind him. Dekker looked down into Kate's worried eyes, then spun around.

"Do me a favor, Sergeant, and back off, see. I'm talking to my wife!" Dekker said calling up his most contemptuous look.

The policewoman with the cool blue eyes stood her ground.

"My name is Sergeant Kitchener to you, Dekker," she said mildly. "Any more rudeness from you, and I will personally de-man you, you wet little sprout."

Dekker stared her down. The sergeant's eyes flicked toward Dupree.

Dekker felt, more than heard, Dupree moving to within strike range behind him.

"Well, at least the mask is off now, Sergeant. All that crap about being a good Englishman and a patriot seems to have disappeared."

The sergeant ignored Dekker; instead, she looked Kate up and down.

"Would you like something to eat, sweetheart? Your husband must get some work done now."

Kate said nothing, just stared into the sergeant's eyes.

"Go, Kate, I'll be fine," Dekker said, "and remember what I said, don't trust a word these people say."

The Sergeant grinned. "Oh tut, tut, Dekker. You really are an arch dramatist, aren't you? Come along, Kate. Dekker may be a brave man, but for all his prodigious intelligence, he does act the fool a bit too often."

"Watch your mouth, Sergeant," Kate said.

This caught the sergeant by surprise. Dekker saw her color rise as she tried to control her temper.

Dekker threw his head back and laughed out loud.

"If this is the worst they've got, we'll be just fine, Kate."

The Sergeant turned smartly on her heel and led Kate from the room.

Dekker eyed Dupree.

"You're a foolish man if you think the sergeant won't even the score. My advice to you is to cooperate and do so fully," Dupree said.

Dekker eyed the solid block of a man confronting him. That accent was familiar . . . French. Dupree was a French name.

"A Frenchman in the English constabulary? There's one for the books," Dekker said.

Dupree smiled wanly. "Not quite. We are a new force. We serve the whole of the EU. And I am Algerian, actually."

"Serve? I see. Tell me, what do they pay you for this kind of service . . . thirty pieces of silver?"

The barb seemed to miss its mark. Dupree simply stared at him.

"What's this all about Dupree. Are we really in danger?"

Silence grew between the two men.

"We need you to read and ask questions. We don't need you mobile; in fact, it would be to our advantage if you were not mobile," Dupree said in his most matter-of-fact tone.

The men stared at each other.

"Am I to take it that we are not free to leave? Lord Ashworth, I presume is good for his word?"

"Lord Ashworth has a job to do and he will do it," Dupree said in his clipped accent.

Dekker looked deep into those coal black eyes and knew he was dealing with a killer.

"We will have your cooperation, no?" Dupree said.

Dekker swallowed hard.

"Lead on, Dupree," he said quietly. "I'll do as you ask if Kate remains safe."

Dupree smiled. Dekker noticed that he had a perfect row of front teeth. Just a little too regular and white to be real.

Chapter 7

Dekker was ushered along a dimly lit corridor. With each tread the floorboards gave off a muffled creak under the thick Persian runner. At the end of the corridor, the two men mounted a grand Victorian-era staircase to a well-lit first floor and stepped onto a thickly carpeted landing. Dupree led Dekker to the right and stopped before a solid-looking oak door. The policeman tapped lightly, then entered.

The men stepped into a large room with high French windows, thickly draped on either side. The curtains had been slightly opened, letting in a thin spill of autumn sunshine. In the center of the room stood Lord Ashworth and a tall man in a shapeless dark suit wearing large, teardrop glasses. The glasses flashed opaque in the light as he looked up from the third man, who was seated at the desk.

Dekker recognized the seated figure right away: his old teacher, Professor Whitely. A feeling of shock overtook him as he walked slowly toward the seated figure. This was Whitely, but somehow profoundly altered . . . those eyes so deep and desolate. A slow, ironic smile stole over Whitely's face as Dekker drew up to the table. Whitely's eyes did not waver as Dekker looked down into his face.

"Professor Whitely?" Dekker said quietly.

"Ah, Dekker, so glad you have come," interrupted Lord Ashworth, in his rotund Oxford accent, as if Dekker had just now arrived at a dinner party thrown in his honor. Dekker looked at Lord Ashworth with undisguised contempt.

Lord Ashworth smiled his pasty smile. "Doctor Sikes, this young man is Dr. Dekker. He prefers just Dekker for one or other reason. Too many Hollywood movies perhaps. Dekker, this is Dr. Sikes, Whitely's treating psychiatrist."

Dekker dimly recognized Sikes. He too was a personality seen on TV from time to time. Dekker recalled him being involved with some sort of chemical rehabilitation of criminals. Another UN/EU flunkey.

"Dr. Sikes, if you please, could you bring Dekker up to speed?"

Dr. Sikes cleared his throat, looking down his long nose at Dekker. Dekker stood his ground, his head bent slightly forward, his brow furrowed, and his eyes turned up toward Sikes. He was not going to make this easy or comfortable for these men. He did not smile or encourage Sikes in any way.

Sikes looked at Lord Ashworth, the beginnings of discomfort showing in a frown.

Lord Ashworth's mouth twitched with a wry smile.

"Come, Dekker. No need for all this pouting. We are all on the same team here . . . Dr. Sikes, if you please?"

"Ah, yes, well to cut a long story short, Whitely here was doing some research for the government and, ah, about a week ago, in the early morning of Friday last, to be precise, while working with some of these, ah, cuneiform tablets," he indicated a table to the far left, "his team had unearthed in the ruins of Babylon—Whitely seems to have suffered some sort of, ah, well, nervous breakdown or some such related illness, er, condition." continued Sikes.

Dekker's eyes flicked to the small table momentarily. Under one of the windows with the bright pearly sunlight lay a neat row of ancient clay tablets. Coming in from the corridor and being forced to look into the light, he had not noticed them.

"You see, he has not stopped talking in what we, er, believe to be ancient Babylonian or Sumerian dialect ever since the—breakdown, and, ah, wisely, Lord Ashworth has brought in your skills to try to help us make some sense of his . . . condition."

Dekker nodded his head and looked down at the old professor. He was fond of Whitely, and they had had a good relationship while he studied at Cambridge.

"So, this is the top secret mission, Lord Ashworth? To rescue an old man from a mental breakdown?"

Ashworth looked furious, but said nothing for a few moments.

"Yes, Dekker, that and the thing Professor Whitely was working on . . . very important. I want a complete and unadulterated version of the conversation you have with Whitely. Is that understood?"

Dekker smiled. "What's the magic word Lord Ashworth?"

"Why, abracadabra, I think?" said Ashworth, turning to Dr. Sikes with a wry smile. Dr. Sikes did not smile.

"Very droll, but you know less drama and a 'please' every now and again would not go astray. May I?" Dekker asked and pulled up a chair, ignoring Lord Ashworth's mounting color.

"Please . . . do," Dr. Sikes said.

Lord Ashworth, Dr. Sikes, and Dupree all moved away. Lord Ashworth poured himself a whiskey from the decanter at the far end of the library, rudely Dekker thought, not offering the other men a drink. Dekker sat down opposite the professor and looked into the familiar face before him. All this time, the professor's gaze had not wavered and neither had the ironic smile.

Yes, definitely the old prof., he thought, *but altered. His features seem leaner, somehow hollow, and the eyes—the pupils almost completely dilated, like he is on a drug.*

The old eyes held a baffling look of pity in them, or derision. The features that Dekker noted were not still. Most particularly, the eyes seemed to alternate between a look of profound fear and haughty derision, but without so much as a flicker of the muscles in the face.

"Professor Whitely?" Dekker spoke softly again. Slowly, he reached over and put his hand gently onto the professor's. Whitely's hand was ice cold.

Suddenly, the old face before him lit up and the most astonishingly fluent Babylonian Dekker had ever heard gushed from the stretched-dry lips in guttural spurts.

As Dekker listened, the other men in the room saw his expression change from surprise to shock, as his naturally ruddy face paled visibly.

"Dekker? Dekker! What is it? What is Whitely saying?" snapped Lord Ashworth.

Suddenly, a hideous wail broke from the old man's throat, long and high. Saliva gushed from the right corner of his mouth. In English, Whitely cried out: "Dekker, for God's sake, don't . . ." then in quavering Babylonian, "Don't let them know. Don't. They mean to use this thing for great evil!"

A sort of punctured gasp ended this sentence, and the maniacal, ironic smile snapped into place again.

Dekker looked into Ashworth's bulging eyes. Incandescent anger seethed through his body. He knew his own face would not hide his emotion; he could hardly control himself. He could see that Ashworth understood the tone of the conversation, if not its content. What had he stumbled into? And he stupidly had now endangered Katie.

"Well, what did the old coot say?"

Dekker gave Ashworth a withering look and said nothing. Dekker knew now that he had made a bad mistake. He resolved to walk out of here as soon as he could.

"I see," said Ashworth quietly. "Let me remind you that we hold your wife in custody."

Dekker looked up at his captors stonily.

"Talk, Dekker! What did that old fool say? Where is it?"

Chapter 8

Obrahim cantered his horse along the high road from the new Sumerian capital of Israel. He could feel the heat radiating from the golden orb in his saddlebag. The horse beneath him skittered and jumped at shadows in the high moonlit night. The mount that trailed behind voiced her displeasure, too, with frequent, uncomfortable whinnying.

The priest did not feel comfortable either. Memories of standing on the burning hill with his queen kept flashing through his mind.

Jezebel, high priestess of Baal, had stepped toward the still burning furnace of the mountain with a look of contempt on her face, orb in hand, a large orb about the size of an adult's head.

Obrahim admired her courage. He cowered in the background, his legs visibly shaking beneath him.

"My Queen, take care! This is holy ground." He heard the tremor in his own voice and felt shame.

"Obrahim, you are weak, and your weakness you will pay for dearly. You will do as your Queen commands." Jezebel's eyes seemed to glow in the firelight and that voice, not her own; she was now filled with the spirit of Baal, more priestess than queen.

"Don't!" shouted Obrahim as Jezebel stepped into the thick stream of molten rock that oozed over the mountain. The sound of high triumphant laughter broke the night air as she bent down and plunged the golden orb deep into the stream of burning stone. The clothes on her body smoldered and then caught fire and burned from her body, leaving her completely naked. Obrahim looked on in horror. Still, she continued until she had filled the golden orb with the flames that had come from Heaven.

Somehow, the fire had not burned her. Obrahim fell to his knees. He had dared not look up into that wild face or look upon her naked form. She was scarcely human. His body shook violently. Obrahim saw her bare feet before him, flames licking the flesh and yet she did not burn and then the orb with its lid firmly screwed into place.

"Take this, faithful Obrahim; along with the sealed tablets you will find in your saddlebag. Go; take this to the high priest of Babylon. The one they call Shumash will know what to do with it," said Jezebel in her strange cracked voice.

"My Queen, what of you? Please, use my cloak."

Obrahim heard the quiet laughter above his head.

"The eunuch below holds a cloak for your Queen. Do as I say. The Baal has spoken great things. You are to be the instrument of his greatest triumph—revenge! Revenge on the House of Israel and upon the Lord of Heaven. Baal will turn Heaven's weapon against itself. Do not ask questions faithful Obrahim, these are things too deep for us to penetrate. Go immediately."

Jezebel signaled to the eunuch below them. He came forward eagerly with a cloak, his greedy eyes taking in the naked form of the queen.

"Makir, do you know the scribe Shelomo?"

"I know of him. He is an old man now."

"You speak more wisely than you know," said the voice of the prophetess.

Makir, the eunuch, laid the cloak gently over the queen's shoulders and bowed.

"Shelomo has seen too many days. He must not see another."

"Yes, my Queen," said the eunuch in his high girlish voice.

Obrahim shivered at this memory. Her voice terrified him, that voice that seemed to travel from far away over the wastes of the desert before it formed in his queen's mouth.

A day or two, he thought, *and I will be safely in Babylon.*

The pounding of horse's hooves off in the distance echoed up the narrow wadi, breaking into his thoughts. Who else but robbers would be traveling this late at night?

Pulling his horse up, he looked around feverishly, then dismounted. He led both horses to a nearby rock fall. The drumbeat of the hooves grew nearer. Whoever traveled this late at night traveled in haste. Obrahim scrambled over the rocks into a small clearing. He held his snorting horses by their bridles and pulled their heads down so that they would not whinny their defiance to the strange horses, which came toward them at a fast canter. The mystery rider and his horses passed by, their hooves a rhythm of sound. At least three or four horses—who could it be?

Obrahim waited for several moments. When he was sure he was alone, he scrambled up to the nearest rock and quickly climbed the rough wadi cliff face. They were near the end of the gully. It was steep and heavy going, but once he gained the top, he had an uninterrupted view of the pale desert sand below him and the curve of the road, which led to Babylon.

The moon rode high that night as the ancient stars shone in all their splendor, but Obrahim's gaze was fixed on the road. Out of the gully and into the plain beyond, a lone rider cantered his horse with several more mounts following behind. This rider, whoever he was, was making great haste to Babylon. Obrahim was not able to recognize the rider from this distance, but there was no doubting the livery that flashed silver on the racing mounts. It was the royal livery. Those horses belonged to the king. But who? Did the king know of Jezebel's plans?

Obrahim thought carefully. Perhaps it was some other business. The scribe had been taking dispatches when they first arrived . . . but why this race to Babylon? The road to Jerusalem went west, not east, of Samaria. Perhaps they were on their way to Petra to trade, but why in the middle of the

The Flame of Heaven

night and why with such haste? No, something was afoot. Perhaps a spy in the court had got wind of Jezebel's plan. It occurred to him that if he could catch this rider, he would probably also catch the man who had told Elijah of Jezebel's departure. Obrahim's mind whirled. His thoughts turned to the tablets, newly pressed and wrapped in sealed clay and leather in his saddlebag—should he read them? He knew it would be an act of disobedience, but he also knew how treacherous Jezebel could be. A strong feeling of terror and great evil came over him as he thought this. The memory of that voice speaking through the queen kept him in fear. She was a prophetess. He dared not defy her; he was an instrument in the hands of the great Baal. He knew beyond doubt that he was in a snare. No matter how much he smarted under the oppression, his own will would not function.

After a long pause, his mind in a fury of thought, he began to climb back down the wadi cliff-face like an old man, making slow progress. He had no doubt that the letter would contain an instruction to kill him—or worse—should the letter arrive at its destination with the seal broken. And who was the mystery rider? Whoever he was, one thing became clear to Obrahim: he was alone and he was a sacrifice, expendable, like all small men in history. Well, he would not play by the rules!

Mind racing, he mounted his horse once more and cantered through the night. He must try to catch up with the rider; the less time he gave his adversaries to think, the better his chances of survival.

ೂಲ್ ೂಲ್ ೂಲ್

On the second night in the desert, he woke in fright, the dregs of his dream fading from his mind. He dreamed that he had been confined in a small dark space for years and years without number. Obrahim gulped greedy lungfuls of air, trying to steady his nerves. Tears started in his eyes as he looked into the star-studded night sky.

A dark shape loomed over him and nudged his head. Terror broke like a wave over his mind. Then, he realized it was his horse.

"Curse you!" he screamed. "Curse you all to Sheol!" Hot tears coursed down his cheeks and into his beard.

The horse started and whinnied her displeasure at his sudden cursing.

He felt trapped as in the flow of a fast-running river, unable to escape or use his own will. His fevered mind wondered precisely when he had become this god's slave.

Chapter 9

Dekker and Kate sat on the edge of a double bed in a quiet room on the west side of the house. It must have been a storeroom or some such thing in times gone by. One small high window on the western wall let in the dying rays of the sun.

"Katie, don't look at me that way. I had to do it. Lord Ashworth threatened to loose that animal, Dupree, on you if I did not cooperate. And besides which, that voice—the one that does not belong to Whitely—has not exactly told me where this mysterious object is. It asks the questions, and I answer. It seems very interested in Lord Ashworth himself."

"Are you saying that the professor is possessed in some way, Dekker?"

"I don't know. I know this sounds like a superstitious piece of mumbo jumbo, except that I saw him myself. And the Babylonian; I mean it's faultless, much better than mine."

Dekker looked thoughtful for a second. "If it is all some sort of elaborate setup, well, why? Why would they do something like that? No, Ashworth is scared. He believes there is something significant here and I don't blame him."

Katie looked at her husband's tired unshaven face. He was not a believer—she knew that. He was a skeptic by nature.

"An object of power? A man possessed? Surely not? Not in the twenty-first century," Dekker said to himself. "I swear, if this was not happening to me I'd scarcely believe it. Am I truly supposed to believe this is the ghost of King Tut or something?"

Kate grinned at him and put a hand on his cheek.

"The spiritual realm is real. You know that, though you try to deny it. God is real and his adversary is real. Why would these people be prepared to do such wicked things if this, this . . . object had no power? And the poor old professor—what is to become of him? His personality has obviously been suppressed by this . . . person. Did it say who it was?"

"No, it, whatever or whomever it is, is very imperious and very angry. Like I said, it asks the questions."

"But the professor, he managed to warn you. I think you should take that warning seriously. Who knows how much courage or strength that took?"

Dekker shivered slightly.

"We're effectively prisoners, and I am powerless to do anything except cooperate at this stage, and that really grates me!" he said.

Katie rubbed her hands over her eyes and down her cheeks, trying to make sense of it all.

"Dekker, there are worse things than dying an honorable death. We're doing wrong. We should not cooperate with this thing. It is evil. I know it."

"Katie, please, no more!" Dekker said sharply. "You don't know what you're asking me to do. They will harm you. I'm not prepared to let that happen. They can have their object or whatever it is. It's probably nothing, anyway. Just some Babylonian cult material that has someone with an over realized view of the occult all excited!"

Kate looked at her husband. Tears suddenly welled in her eyes.

"I've been praying. I've been praying nonstop since we were taken. You know I'm sure the Lord hears our prayers. There is something terribly evil . . ."

Dekker took her hand and squeezed it. "Shush, Katie. That's why I love you, Kate. That strength to believe in the . . . providence of God. You know, the thing is, maybe God just means that we should muddle through this as best we can. After all, we don't really know what's going on. Give me more time. Let me find out what's really going on, and then I'll be able to make up my mind as to whether a sacrifice is necessary. Okay?"

Now tears welled in his eyes, and he wiped at them quickly with his free hand.

There was a sharp knock on the door, and then a head pushed through.

"Come on, lovebirds," said the sergeant, in an overly cheerful manner. "Suppertime, and then I'm afraid, Dekker, you have to get back to work."

ತಿ⊸ ತಿ⊸ ತಿ⊸

At the dinner table the mood was subdued. Lord Ashworth sat at the head, Sibyl to his right, and to his left, the sergeant. Dekker and Katie sat opposite each other. Dekker noted that Dupree sat next to Katie, presumably to keep him in line should he rebel.

"So, Kate I understand you are an accountant and that you, er work from home?" said Sibyl.

"Interesting that you should know so much about me. Did you say anything about my vocation to these friendly people, Dekker?" Katie said lightly.

Sibyl's face suffused with disbelief. She glanced at Lord Ashworth.

"Mmm, let me see," Dekker said, sarcastically, "I don't recall talking about your job, I rather thought it was my job we were talking about."

"I'm amazed at your effrontery," Katie said directly to Sibyl, her eyes taking in Lord Ashworth in the same violent sweep.

The two of them looked stolidly at Dekker and Katie.

"I think what Sibyl was trying to convey to you, Kate, was that we would be willing to pick some work up for you should you wish us to, so that you would not fall behind," Lord Ashworth said firmly.

"You mean, Lord Ashworth, that my job is a loose end and my agent might try to get hold of me if I don't return my work on time? Mmm, too kind. No, on second thought I think I'll let them wonder."

Katie turned to Dupree and added, "Make yourself useful, monkey, and pass me the beans please."

Dupree obeyed reluctantly.

Dekker chuckled under his breath and felt very proud of his wife.

Sibyl cracked a smile. "A spirited lass I see. But high spirits can be broken easily enough, God knows. Since you lack manners, I'll give it to you in a vulgar dialect you'll understand. We have taken the liberty of retrieving your computer, we know what kind and volume of work your agent is expecting of you, and we will even allow you a monitored use of the phone if need be. You will deliver your work as normal."

"And if I don't?"

"Then, my dear, we will make sure you have a verifiable medical reason not to," Sibyl said acidly.

Dupree's hands dropped from view.

A slow flush rose over Dekker's cheeks. He gripped his knife and speedily calculated if he would be able to lunge at Dupree's jugular from where he sat.

"Dekker, don't bother. Dupree has his gun trained on you under the table," said Katie, her color up.

Dekker stared into Dupree's eyes, then said very slowly: "Dupree, I want you to know that I am going to kill you."

Dupree smiled but said nothing, his eyes pits of hate.

Katie pushed her chair back and got up. "Excuse me," she said, "the company leaves me feeling sick. I think I'll go back to our room. Dekker, would you mind . . ."

Dekker smiled at her, "Not at all, my dear, since the pretense that we ever possessed freedom is now at an end. Lord Ashworth, you are a man of law? What section are we being held under?"

Dekker rose and Dupree rose with them, his gun out of its holster against his thigh.

Lord Ashworth sighed dramatically. "All so unnecessary. Dupree, see them to their room and lock the door after them. Their manners will no doubt improve with their appetites. As for the section of the law I hold you under young Dekker . . . well I call it Section D. That section stands for, 'do as I say'."

Sibyl's rasping laughter and Sergeant Kitchener's sycophantic whinny accompanied them back to their room.

Lord Ashworth's merciless eyes followed the young couple from the room.

"You know sergeant, I do believe I have made a tactical error," he said.

"What makes you say that Lord Ashworth?" said Sergeant Kitchener brightly.

"That young woman is definitely giving our good Dr. Dekker courage. He is a different man around her. I think we will separate them."

The two women looked at each other and smiled.

Chapter 10

Though his thoughts weighed heavily in his mind, Obrahim always loved the approach to the Great City. Babylon was not the capital of the Assyrian empire, Nineveh to the north was the capital, but for all her beauty Nineveh could not rival her sister's greatness and beauty. They were undiminished despite the fact that Babylon now wore the yoke of Assyrian oppression. Before your eyes ever saw her, you knew you approached a magnificent city. The dust kicked up by the many pilgrims who came to worship at her temples and trade in her marketplaces rose to Heaven like incense. This you saw from a great distance away, then the outlying fields of yellow barley and the great canals spread out like a hand from the river Euphrates, some so large that one could see the sails of boats, floating as if by magic, above the vast fields.

As Obrahim traveled a little further, there rose before him her enormous ziggurat, Babylon's mighty walls, and the glistening ribbon of the Euphrates River itself winding through her carefully tilled fields. Obrahim let his tired mounts nose their way through the nearest field of barley to a craftily dug canal, this one but a mere three feet wide. The priest's intelligent eyes took in the engineering feat and noted how the water was ingeniously piped from the canal to water the whole field.

Babylon was a great oasis in the desert, and the people flocked to her in the thousands to buy and sell whatever was needful. Babylon the Great—she was well named.

The Flame of Heaven

The ziggurat to the god Marduk, at the center of the city, loomed before Obrahim like a great mountain on the flood plain of the Euphrates. Obrahim was comforted knowing that Marduk was none other than Baal by a different name. Before you ever saw those impressive walls, it was the temple mound of Marduk that first greeted the weary traveler from afar. The great worship center of Baal Bek in Sidonia and the priests of Babylon worked together and had a network of informants that was legendary. Try as he might, he had not been able to penetrate Babylon's network in the court at Samaria, but he had no doubt it existed. No doubt Queen Jezebel knew who those informants were. It was rumored that she had her own network of spies in the region. He'd never trusted those eunuchs. They were too near the women of the court and there was something quite unnatural about them; they were sly.

His mind slid back to the present. There was no need to fret. The real power was Marduk or Baal. Even from a great distance you could see the date palms clinging to the side of the ziggurat. The closer one came, the more breathtaking the sight. Babylon's famous turquoise-tiled walls glittered like cool water in the harsh sun.

ชิ∘๙ ชิ∘๙ ชิ∘๙

Obrahim entered the western gate, Ishtar by name, along the Processional Way on a hard bitumen road that led into the heart of the city. The walls of the Ishtar gate were decorated with dark blue tiles and the motif of the dragon serpent and bull god in gold. The gate itself soared like a wadi on each side of his mount, at least three chariot spans wide. Soldiers in their glittering bronze mail, headgear, and scarlet cloaks patrolled the towers above the gate and the gate itself.

On his approach to the gate the traffic slowed. Obrahim noted that soldiers were collecting tax from other travelers who intended to sell their goods in the city—*a lucrative little trade*, he thought to himself. He was not about to be dunned.

One soldier let the haft of his spear fall before Obrahim's mount.

"What is your business in Babylon?" the soldier said, eyeing the saddlebags on his horses.

"My business is with the high priest of Marduk himself, the priest Shumash," Obrahim said, his eyes fierce with haughty indignation.

The soldier looked him over, his eyes assessing the likely veracity of such a story, resting on the quality of Obrahim's tunic and cloak and the workmanship of his horse's saddle and bridle. Although he was travel stained and weary, Obrahim knew the young soldier would think very carefully before offending the high priest's guest.

"If you intend to trade, you must pay a gate tax," the soldier said, eyeing him speculatively.

Obrahim's temper was sorely tested; an honest man in Babylon was hard to find.

"I have not come to trade."

"Open your saddlebags," the soldier said and prodded the nearest bag with the butt end of his spear.

"Stop, you fool! That saddlebag contains a gift for the high priest," Obrahim cried.

The soldier stepped back, flustered at Obrahim's anger. The commotion attracted the attention of the guards on the gate towers. Obrahim saw their conical copper helmets gleaming in the sunshine as they looked down upon the scene.

"What's going on here, then?" an authoritative voice boomed out.

Obrahim turned to see the captain, dressed in blue and gold, making his way toward them.

"This fool is going to destroy the high priest's gift, a gift from none other than the Queen of Israel!"

"You are a representative of the Queen?" the captain said. Obrahim heard the doubtful tone of the question. "Then, where is your retinue? Do you have letters of introduction?"

Before Obrahim could answer the captain said, "Off your horse, old man. Let us have a look in those bags."

The Flame of Heaven

"I warn you, this is not something you should meddle in captain," Obrahim said. By now, quite a crowd had gathered around Obrahim. He got off his horse.

"Open the saddlebag." The captain pointed to the bag containing the orb.

"You open it. There is a magical gift inside, and it will surely destroy the one who touches it."

The captain laughed scornfully, "A likely story . . . you priests and your omens. I have never met a priest yet who tells the truth."

The captain indicated to the soldier that he should open the saddlebag.

The soldier unbound the saddlebag, and it fell to the ground with a dull metallic thud. Smirking, the soldier opened it, and upended the contents onto the bitumen.

"An incense burner? Perhaps you are telling the truth. Check what is inside the burner," the captain said with a shrewd look on his blunt face.

"This would not be the first time someone had tried to smuggle precious stones or silver into Babylon without paying the requisite tax."

The soldier picked up the orb, a frown on his face, and shook it.

"What?" the captain asked, looking at the soldier's expression.

"It is very heavy, Captain, and quite hot."

A wicked smile spread over Obrahim's face. "I have warned you, captain, the consequences are yours alone."

The captain eyed Obrahim; he disliked priests in general. They were a lazy bunch as far as he was concerned, but he disliked this priest in particular. He had the haughty attitude that men of action despise in the intelligentsia.

"Aargh!" the soldier screeched and suddenly dropped the orb. He raised roasted hands to the captain, a look of astonished pain etched into his face. "Quick! Water!" The soldier pranced around with his burned hands before his face, screaming for help. Some quick-thinking bystander poured a gourd of water over the soldier's hands, and he was led away moaning pitifully.

Obrahim laughed at the soldier's distress.

The anger and indignation in the captain had turned to genuine fear. Clearly this was a man of power, possessed by a god.

"Go, priest," the captain said evenly. He could not hold Obrahim's eye. Turning his back on the scene, he walked away with stiff legs toward the guardhouse.

Obrahim looked at the other soldiers present.

"Do any of you care to inspect my saddlebags further?" he said.

None of them was man enough to make eye contact with him.

"Oh, do please," he said through a sneer. He bent down and picked up the orb in one fluid motion. The soldiers looked to see if he would burn, but he did not. Obrahim's luminous eyes searched out the eyes of the young soldier standing nearest him. The soldier shuddered involuntarily. Obrahim smiled, then mounted his horse and noted with satisfaction the wide berth given to him and his horses as he entered Babylon.

Respect . . . that was what was missing. No one, not even the Queen, showed him enough respect.

Suddenly, the fear that had ridden with him all the way from Samaria fell away. It was as if the incense burner, in his own mind he had begun to call it the Flame of Heaven, had set him free. The irony of this situation did not pass through his mind unnoticed. The very God of Israel he had so despised had set him free from the chains that Baal had manacled him with.

He probed his own mind tentatively. Miraculously free! The feeling of oppression had simply vanished.

And now, he thought to himself, *I am sick of being the plaything of the gods. I will go my own way. It is time to pay my Queen back with her own coin.*

If Obrahim had not been so preoccupied with his own thoughts his quick eyes would probably have noticed the middle-aged man following him. The same man whose actions had saved the burned hands of the young soldier when he had poured water onto them—Shelomo the scribe, whom Jezebel said should never see another day, well known in the right circles as one of Babylon's most gifted scribes—followed Obrahim at a discrete distance. His nondescript Semitic appearance, dark skin, long oiled beard and hair worn long in the Babylonian fashion, helped him to blend in. Only his eyes would have set him apart. They were afire with intelligence and darted to and fro, absorbing information. He wore a regulation length white kaftan and carried a short brass walking stick, which to a practiced eye marked him as a man employed by the Temple complex. This man followed Obrahim into the coppersmith quarter of the city. A large trade in copper goods went on in the labyrinthine streets of the smithing quarter, full of smoke and steam and the incessant din of the smithing and the bustle of the trade. *A good place to lose a tail, thought Shelomo*, but it could work both ways.

Shelomo ducked behind a pile of kettles suspended from the rafters of a stall as Obrahim threw a nonchalant glance behind him before dismounting his horse. He took the saddlebag containing the orb from the horse's saddle and walked into a shop. The shop housed one of Babylon's finest metal smith workshops, but it was small and nondescript on the outside. His heart skipped a beat. He could not believe his good fortune. He knew the proprietor very well—Marook—a gifted man. Most of the high priest's implements were crafted in this workshop, and it was he, Shelomo, who usually paid for the order. Shelomo smiled to himself—*the nondescript appearance was probably the reason why Obrahim had chosen it, though surely Providence must play a part.*

Shelomo was impressed at how quickly Obrahim had covered the distance between Ahab's court and Babylon. He himself had pushed his mounts hard, and despite having two more horses to draw from, he had only arrived in Babylon a day and a night ahead of Obrahim. That could only mean one thing; Obrahim had pushed his mounts because the priest of Baal must have known someone else was on the road. The letter itself to Shumash was not urgent, although the instructions were exact and very important. It was this tone of patience that had disturbed him and Elijah the most.

His vigilance had paid off. Spying in any court was dangerous, but spying in the court of King Ahab was especially treacherous, with Queen Jezebel around in a murderous mood. His position as a retired scribe and lowly messenger at the Samarian court had allowed him to go unnoticed and to keep tabs on Jezebel as well as communicate with the people of God. He had also kept careful watch on the eunuchs. Their circle had proved much more difficult to penetrate than the prophets of Baal.

Shelomo knew he would never be able to return to the court of King Ahab again. He knew too much and his unthinking action in saving the young soldier's hands would have ensured that Obrahim had noticed him, and that would mean his usefulness to Shumash, the chief priest in Babylon, would be limited. *He would have to leave soon*, he thought.

His practiced eye flicked over Obrahim's mounts. They looked dead on the hoof and one of them was limping badly. The poor faithful beast's next stop would probably be the slaughterhouse. Shelomo sidled around the back of the metal smith's shop. The shop front made up the first floor of a two-story mud, brick, and straw dwelling. At the back of the home was a staircase, which led to the upper story. He looked over his shoulder; no one had seen him. He saw only women with their jars and children playing in the street with their tethered animals. The din of the city and the usual domestic sounds washed over the alley. He made his way quickly up the stairwell and knocked on the wooden door. It opened a crack; the pair of eyes which confronted him were feminine and wary.

"Shelomo, how good to see you, here let me undo the hitch."

"Good woman, do not. I only have a moment. There is a strange man in your husband's workshop. He has an incense burner with him. He is no doubt looking for an incense burner like the one that he has. He must be followed and I must know what he does with the burner in his possession. This is most important."

The woman's eyes widened fractionally, and then she nodded.

"Please let your husband know what I have said. I must not be missed at the Temple. I must go now."

With that Shelomo turned on his heel.

Chapter 11

The guards at the entrance to the massive temple complex surrounding the ziggurat seemed less than impressed at Obrahim's credentials. They had merely taken his letter to a waiting eunuch while he, Obrahim, was made to kick his heels in one of the many temple antechambers. After a period of waiting, which seemed an affront, a young eunuch boy led him through a quiet section of the temple to some rooms and a washhouse. He had anticipated subtle insults, but thankfully the room was not a shared accommodation. At the washhouse, he had received his due, a thorough scrub by a rather heavyset bath attendant and a good oiling down of his skin. He started to relax. He had taken some precautions that would, he thought to himself, at least ensure his survival and this rubdown was good. He might even go and relieve himself with a temple prostitute.

"That will be three shekels," wheezed the bath attendant after the last slap of oil.

"What!" exclaimed Obrahim, apoplectic with rage. "Do you know who I am?" he said, his voice rising.

The bath attendant looked at him blandly, his jowls wobbled slightly, and he took three labored breaths. "If you do not have the money," he said, his little pig eyes not leaving Obrahim's, "you will be imprisoned."

The obscene jowls wobbled again as he motioned to a guard, a large, surly individual, none too bright looking with a

The Flame of Heaven

shaved head. Obrahim was experienced enough to know that there was no reasoning with the guard.

"I will have to go to my room to retrieve the money," he spat.

He walked with a stiff gait and all the dignity he could muster, every fiber of his being pulsating with fury, the guard loping behind him. He conducted an enraged search for his purse. He found it and extracted the silver needed. That sum would have paid an average worker for a month. He walked back to the bathhouse and got within range of the attendant.

"Here, you corpulent pig!" he screamed and flung the silver at the face of the still phlegmatic man. The attendant must have been used to this sort of outrage from strangers, for he simply stepped aside and the fragments of metal sailed by harmlessly. Some men and their attendants on the far side of the room grunted their laughter at Obrahim's discomfort.

"The high priest will hear of this!" Obrahim declared. This was not the sort of reception he had been expecting with a letter of introduction from Jezebel herself, a well-respected figure among the Babylonian priesthood.

Back in his room he dressed quickly and stomped off to the reception area. He would see the high priest immediately!

"I'm sorry the high priest is not available immediat . . ."

"Immediately!" Obrahim shouted, spittle flecking the face of the young priest.

An audience quickly sought would give the priests of Marduk less time to prepare the plot he knew must come. Still, they had had plenty of time to prepare.

The young priest at the entrance to the high priest's chambers bowed diffidently to Obrahim.

"You may enter now."

Obrahim walked through the beautifully tiled antechamber into the high priest's private rooms. The glare of midday light was mercifully suffused here and highlighted the beautifully whorled carvings in the stone window coverings. Deep blue silk curtains hung from the ceiling. High color in his cheeks was the only sign left of the outrage he felt at the impudent way he had been treated by the guards and the temple officials.

Shumash would hear of this outrage and none too subtly either.

As Obrahim's eyes adjusted to the light, he made out a tall, big-boned figure standing in the shadow of one of the large, blue curtains, the outline of the great curved headwear etched by fractured light.

A heavyset eunuch appeared from a room to the right of Obrahim. In the distinctive boy's voice of the eunuch, he bid Obrahim be seated before a low table on a couch, poured spiced wine into a silver goblet that stood on the table, and then set an earthenware bowl of dates and a small, delicate-looking red fruit before him. Obrahim eyed them hungrily. He had never seen such fruit before. Shumash moved from the window and seated himself on the other side of the table. Dignity was of the utmost importance in such meetings.

Not wanting to appear greedy or ignorant, Obrahim picked up the goblet and drained it. He was parched from his travels, and although he had drunk deeply from the cistern in his room, the wine quenched an altogether different appetite, one that had not been fed for some time. He had only entered Babylon that morning. He managed an appreciative burp for his host.

Shumash smiled his satisfaction.

"Welcome. Obrahim, high priest of Baal. I read the sealed tablets you delivered for your Queen. The communication is a most curious one," Shumash said quietly.

Obrahim looked up into two keen, gray eyes, eerily clear of any fleck or discoloration, the color of the desert sky before a sandstorm and just as menacing. His sense of outrage abated somewhat. He hoped he had made a good first impression, but he was feeling wary, and what he had just endured had not bolstered his pride or his strength.

Obrahim lay back into the couch, watching carefully the movements of Shumash in his long white linen robe. "Your attendants . . ." began Obrahim.

The Flame of Heaven

The high priest made the sound with his mouth of a man passing wind and flicked his hand. "Think no more of such conduct. Even in Babylon it is hard to find men of intelligence."

"The bath attendant charged me three shekels," Obrahim said acidly. He eyed the high priest. He could not tell for sure, but it seemed as if the high priest was struggling to keep from laughter.

"I . . . I will see to it that you are . . . er, recompensed," said the high priest.

Obrahim smiled a self-satisfied smile.

Yes, a little firm resolve worked even here in Babylon and at the highest level. He took a mouthful of the delightful looking red fruit . . . so sweet, but with just a little hint of bitterness as one swallowed. "Most interesting," he said and smiled, then leaned back into the couch.

Shumash waved at the eunuch. The heavy man stepped forward and diffidently adjusted the cushions behind the high priest's back.

"I trust the queen is well?"

"The queen was in fine form when I left her," Obrahim said. He sensed from Shumash's twitch of a smile that his humor had been appreciated. This set Obrahim at his ease, and he took another mouthful of the strange, sweet fruit.

Shumash observed him quietly from the other side of the table.

"The letter made it quite plain that your queen values her servant highly, and she instructed us to treat you with great care."

Now Obrahim smiled openly.

"I trust your rooms are to your satisfaction."

"My room is fine," said Obrahim crisply.

Shumash bowed again.

"My apologies. I will see to it that you are moved into more comfortable quarters."

"Your horses are stabled with the temple?"

"My horses are dog meat by now. I came with all haste and sold them at the meat market this morning. Both of them were lame."

"Then you are a more diligent servant than even your queen knows. I will recompense you with my own stock."

Obrahim smiled a genuine smile now. Shumash seemed genuinely mollified and more importantly off balance.

"The letter also spoke of an object that you carry . . . an orb, a burner? Your queen has instructed you to give it to me for safekeeping. You have it with you?" Shumash made a show of looking into the folds of Obrahim's cloak, though any fool could see that he would not be able to conceal a burner there.

Obrahim's eyes narrowed. "It is an object of great power," he said brusquely. "Forgive me, but my queen gave me no such verbal instruction. I will need to read the letter myself."

A momentary hesitation and a look of . . . was it triumph . . . in the eyes of this Babylonian priest? A tightness, a suppressed glee?

"Forgive me, this is a most unusual communication. I have not told you everything," Shumash said.

"At the bottom of the letter is a code. No key is given for its deciphering. Your queen says in her letter that you possess the key?"

So, Shumash plays games. Well, he cannot win, thought Obrahim. What petty triumph. Frankly, he would be glad to be rid of the tiresome burner—but not just yet. The safety of the orb was now not in question, but his own safety had not been guaranteed; he would see to that first. Once that was done, why, he might even enjoy the spectacle of another bath with the surly bath attendant bowing and scraping and being forced to do his bidding for no pay.

Shumash leaned forward, the tablets in hand, stretching them forward, but just out of reach of Obrahim's outstretched hand. "The orb—is it in your room?"

"What? Such game playing, Shumash," he said with a smile twisting his lips.

Are we children?

The Flame of Heaven

The gray eyes of the chief priest held Obrahim's firmly.

"I will have one of the scribes bring the orb. The letter clearly states . . ."

"Yes, yes of course," Obrahim said, reaching out and at the last second taking a handful of fruit instead of the tablets— the slightest curl of a smile to his lip.

Shumash dropped the tablets between them and indicated that one of the scribes should come forward.

"Shelomo, retrieve the orb from the high priest's room."

Obrahim turned slightly to see the form of Shelomo, the scribe, departing. Something about the scribe made him start. Recognition kindled in him. The way he carried himself, his profile. He had seen Shelomo somewhere before. Or had he? Perhaps his guilty conscience was playing tricks on him. His head felt fuzzy.

Obrahim leaned backward onto the cushions, satisfied that he had the psychological advantage now. He had thought this encounter through carefully. The slights intended to intimidate him and the unpleasant incident clearly meant to unsettle him he had now turned to his advantage.

How amateurish, he thought as he nibbled another of the delicious red fruits.

"The key to the code?" Shumash said.

"If I possess the key, Shumash, then it is a mystery to me. Here, let me have a look." In the corridor beyond the curtain Obrahim vaguely heard the shuffle of feet and whispered voices.

"Master, the orb," came the scribe's deep voice, back from his errand. The scribe placed the orb between the two men on the low table.

Obrahim looked up at the face of the scribe. Yes, he definitely had seen that face before, but could not quite place it— a Semitic face. There were devout Jews who lived among the Babylonians.

The eyes of Shumash were closed doors. The chief priest of Marduk gazed at the orb and then looked steadily into the eyes of the man opposite him.

Obrahim met the gaze. *Maybe, just maybe, this would work*, he thought, *but surely Shumash could not assume that he, Obrahim, would be stupid enough to bring such a prize within the walls of Babylon.*

Everyone knew that all the world's cutthroats, charlatans, and thieves made their way to this place and here, he thought to himself, *I'm merely describing the priests of Babylon. The queen, had she placed a spell on him? Is that why she was so confident of his service?*

His thoughts seemed slow; he leaned further forward.

There was a shuffling of nervous feet behind him.

His mind seemed slow, perhaps fatigue was catching up with him.

Still Shumash gazed at him with that odd look in his eyes. Obrahim picked up the first tablet and read it quickly. At the top of the letter he read the usual greeting to Shumash in Babylonian script, then an explanation of what the orb was and how it was to be kept, and a sentence saying that the queen expected to visit Babylon soon.

Then a paragraph in Persian script—a language he had never learned. This was obviously a private communication between the queen and Shumash. When Obrahim reached these lines, he stopped and looked up into those gray unblinking eyes again. They were giving nothing away—interesting.

Obrahim kept on reading. Another paragraph of Babylonian script described Obrahim himself and his mission. The letter did instruct Obrahim to hand the orb over to Shumash. Obrahim nodded and puckered his mouth.

But then something strange. On the last of the tablets, as Shumash had said, Jezebel had written something about a code that Obrahim possessed with which he could decipher the rest of the letter, but the rest of the letter was not written in code at all. It was written in old Phoenician, a language that Obrahim knew well and presumably Shumash did not. Obrahim had grown up speaking it as a boy on the coast of Lebanon. Jezebel was from the same region of Sidonia. She therefore knew Obrahim would understand this script.

The Flame of Heaven

Obrahim looked up.

Could it be that Shumash was Persian? He was fairly light skinned, unable to read Phoenician, just as he, Obrahim, was unable to read Persian.

His mind seemed suspended, not able to make judgments about these facts. He shook his head trying to clear it. The letter went on.

He read the words in old Phoenician. Right at the bottom of the tablet:

"Obrahim, you are now the guardian of the orb. Baal has made his will clear. You will know when to use its power. Use it to avenge me, your queen, against the God of Israel. Baal has revealed my fate to me . . . and yours."

Obrahim frowned. *Had the queen finally lost her mind?*

Obrahim looked up in the watchful gray eyes. There seemed to be a question hovering in their depths. Obrahim saw them flick down toward the bright red fruits he had been eating and then finally he understood. The fruit was drugged; that was why his mind could not focus. With all his last remaining strength, he drew the curved knife at his side and lunged at those steady gray eyes.

Shumash reeled backwards, his eyes alight with triumph.

Someone screamed behind Obrahim . . . then he saw why. A blue light on the surface of the last tablet pulsed in his hand and raced up his arm. His mind reacted so slowly. What did it mean? He felt the crackle of magic grip his arm as the blue light, like liquid fire, ran up over his chest and onto his face.

The last lines written in only a script he could read . . . of course. The reading of them must have loosed the spell.

From an infinite distance, he heard himself scream. The blue light alive. Such cold pain ran down his face and into his gasping mouth.

Too late to summon his own carefully prepared spell.

The sardonic gray eyes of the high priest opened in surprise. Obrahim looked up at the high priest bent over him. Obrahim could not move.

The cold fire reached into his chest and sucked the wind from his lungs. He tried to drop the tablet, but his hand would not respond to the command in his mind.

The gray eyes, horrified, snapped their attention to the face of the scribe who kept on shouting for Shumash to move away.

"Shut up you fool! I know not to touch him!" Very carefully, Shumash bent over Obrahim.

"Obrahim! Obrahim I had no idea this would happen. Jezebel instructed me to drug you. She said you would be reluctant to part with the orb. This orb, is it the one given to you by Jezebel?"

Through the searing pain, Obrahim managed a last sneer.

"Fool," he spat.

"Where is the orb? Please!" Shumash shouted.

No answer, just a choking splutter from Obrahim, who fought valiantly against the powerful magic of Jezebel.

Shumash turned on the scribe. "You said that you saw him transfer the orb from the saddlebag to his cloak outside the temple, and when he went to bathe, you expressly told me it was in his room!"

"Master, I did not lie. I saw it with my own eyes. This is the one he had in his possession!" Shelomo said.

Laughter welled up in Obrahim's mind. *So elegant, so simple. Well, Jezebel had outsmarted them both, but he knew her for a treacherous witch, and he had taken precautions. He alone knew where the real orb lay. They would never find it in the vastness that was Babylon and they would never think to look there . . .*

The spell ended as abruptly as it had started. Shumash looked with fury at the scattered tablets on the table. The spell was one of occlusion. Obrahim's spirit had been forced from his body into one of the tablets. His body lay like a squeezed-out pomegranate where it fell.

A furious and powerful wizard, in the person of Obrahim, would possess whoever read that tablet next. And when next he possessed a body, there would be no drug to subdue him. Shumash knew without a doubt that the detestable Jezebel had worked her trickery again. No doubt the only instructions on how to use the orb were contained in the coded text. He dared not even look at the tablets, lest his mind form the words and Obrahim come back and possess him. Which tablet possessed the spell was anyone's guess.

He shuddered at the thought. He dared not let another read it; he knew how powerful Obrahim was—that was why they had to drug him. People would die if he was allowed to come back now and the orb lost forever. What a fool he had been!

"This is your fault Shelomo . . . why did I listen to you! Quick, you fool, seal up the tablets and place them in the orb and put it in a safe place within the temple treasury."

"Yes, Master," Shelomo said bowing deeply.

Shumash walked furiously in a circle wringing his hands.

"Shelomo, wait! Once you have taken care of the burner and tablets, be sure to search every inch of Obrahim's possessions. Find his horses wherever they are and cut them into pieces, search their innards, and search every inch of his room and do this yourself . . . quietly. Try to find out where else he has been this day. He only arrived this morning; he could not have attended many places. I do not want word of Obrahim's arrival getting back to the Assyrian spies. Turn every inch of his room inside out. Find out exactly where he has been in Babylon. We must find the real orb!"

"Yes, Master," Shelomo the scribe said and sped away.

Shumash had severely underestimated Obrahim. Still, all was not lost; they must do their best to find the orb. Confound his impudence! How had this man managed to evade him, and what would he tell Queen Jezebel when she came looking for her orb? Even the high priest of Babylon was not safe from the reaches of that witch. She had powerful friends everywhere. If the Assyrians found out that the Babylonians possessed a mighty weapon, and that he, a Persian and a sworn enemy of the Assyrians possessed it, they would show no mercy to their Babylonian servants. Jezebel would have to die, he thought. *No, no, that was unthinkable, but was there any alternative?*

And what of Shelomo? He was an Israelite spy; he had seen everything and knew all the players. Who knows what side he is really on? He would have to die, too. That would be a simpler task than killing Jezebel.

It was all Shelomo's talk of Obrahim being a powerful wizard that had thrown him. In fact, the more he thought about it the more he saw the crafty hand of Shelomo in all of this. It was Shelomo who had somehow had the luck of writing the letter for Jezebel and who had suggested the drug they used to put in the fruit. It was Shelomo who had told him that the orb was in Obrahim's room. For all he knew the scribe who he had inherited from the high priest before his reign could at this very moment be secreting the real orb somewhere. Well, there were ways of making a man tell his secrets. Before he died, Shelomo would reveal all.

Shumash thought furiously. There was someone he could trust.

"Kashka!"

"You called, sire," said the rotund eunuch in his high voice.

Shumash smiled at the eunuch. *That voice had beguiled a few people in its time. It belied a keen intellect and considerable physical strength.*

"Faithful Kashka. You have seen and heard all that has passed here today—keep an eye on Shelomo. I do not want him disappearing before I have had a chance to question him closely."

Kashka bowed deeply, to hide his smile. "Yes, sire. I shall do as you bid."

A wry smile played around Shumash's lips. "Go Kashka and be careful. I have never trusted that Shelomo. A man who can spy on his own people is not a man to be trusted."

Chapter 12

"Come in, Kirsten." She stood on the doorstep of a nondescript town house in Bloomingdale, not far from the museum. Kirsten flashed the older lady a quick smile and stepped through the threshold into a well-lit corridor. The older lady looked out into the quiet street and cast her quick, dark eyes right and left. Nothing moved.

Kirsten turned and stepped through a door midway down the corridor into a large room in which a double bed and a large wooden table stood. In the gloom sat at the table a sturdy, tall, gray-haired male figure with a headphone pressed to his ear, a receiver of some sort with dials waving gently in their electric glow of simulated speech. The figure sat upright when Kirsten entered, his intelligent dark eyes glittering in the dim light.

"Okay, Lewis," he said in his accented English—*Eastern European thought Kirsten.* Though she had heard a great deal about this man over the years, she had never met him.

"Good man. Keep at it, and for Heaven's sake, do not let them even get a hint of your whereabouts. We know where they have them now. Just make sure that if they move them you know about it. Ask Declan to follow anyone who leaves the building."

The needles waved in their static ether again, Lewis responding no doubt, and then fell to zero.

The seamed face of the man smiled at Kirsten and then took off the headphone and microphone.

"Welcome, Kirsten," he said "You have done well. The Cele Dei commends you. Thanks to your good work, we know where Dekker and his wife are being held, and your friends Lewis and Declan are monitoring the property as we speak. It's an old manor property not far from Salisbury."

"Thank you, sir. I did my best. I only hope Dekker and Kate will be okay."

The older man smiled. "My friends call me Shelomo. I think Kirsten, your work at the museum is nearly done. Hand in your resignation and give about four weeks notice. We must be able to leave immediately if necessary."

Kirsten nodded. "To be quite honest with you Shelomo, that Miss Hardacre was starting to grate on my nerves a wee bit. I will not mind leaving. Shall I go and pack up my things at the flat then, and make ready for when we move?"

Shelomo grinned. "Don't worry about your things. The Cele Dei is well provisioned."

Kirsten smiled, remembering. She and her Pa had always lived light, and they had moved around a bit when she was young. When she was old enough she had been told about the Cele Dei, and how this blessed burden passed down in family lines. Soon she would have to make a choice, her father had said, to be part of this great and ancient group of believers, or to stop the Dunnbar line. She had chosen to go on and as Shelomo smiled up at her, she knew in her heart that she had made the right choice.

Chapter 13

Dekker's mind raced as they strode the stairs back to the library. He and Kate had been left in the room for a good hour and he had to admit, however reluctantly, that Lord Ashworth was right; hunger would eventually force them to cooperate. He was already ravenous. To Dekker's amazement, the sergeant had opened the door to their room unannounced and said that she intended to take them shopping tomorrow. Not of course in London. That probably would have been too dangerous in that there was the slightest possibility of running into someone they knew, but Salisbury, the nearest, reasonably-sized town.

"You'll need supplies, clothing and the like. You understand that we cannot risk you going back to your own flat . . . surveillance and all that."

It was at this point that Dekker had finally had enough and firmly resolved in his own mind that he would do his best to smash this ring of intrigue. Kate's show of courage at dinner had done its work. She had been magnificent.

"Pray tell, Sarg., who might you be expecting to be watching my flat?"

No answer, just a withering cold stare.

"Dekker, please. Please believe us. This is a most important project, and we are not the only ones who are after this artifact. It is most valuable. As I have said, it is of international importance that our side 'wins' this little tussle."

"What is this artifact you go on about? That thing inside the professor, whatever it is, is not exactly cooperating, you know. To be quite frank, Sarg, if you want my cooperation, the least you could do is tell me what the hell I'm looking for."

That had ended the conversation abruptly, and the rest of the hour passed without them being disturbed. A tense quiet seemed to grip the manor house.

The sergeant came for Dekker. Kate was left in the room with a book, and Dekker and the sergeant returned to the library. Dekker noted that the sergeant, who had gone ahead, now cleared a half-eaten supper from the table in front of the professor and left abruptly.

The professor himself was on his feet looking out of the window into the night, his hands behind his back. Without his turning around, the cracked dry voice that was not the professor's broke from his throat.

"Tell Lord Ashworth that we are being observed."

"What?" Dekker answered in Babylonian.

"Tell him that there is someone watching this dwelling," said the voice.

Dekker's mind reeled. Could it be that Lord Ashworth was telling the truth after all?

"Tell him!" The voice came harsh and forbidding.

"What is he saying?" asked Lord Ashworth.

"He, he says," said Dekker, hesitantly, "that we are being watched. This house is being watched."

Lord Ashworth's eyebrows arched, and his mouth formed a bemused smile.

"Oh! Are we now. How very interesting." Lord Ashworth flipped open his cell phone. "Yes, Sergeant, I think we have company. Secure the house, get some backup and bring dogs. They are most useful in moments like this. They will give us the advantage in the dark."

He listened for a moment, "Yes, yes, I know it will take some time to organise."

Closing his cell phone, he turned once more to Dekker. "Please thank him for me."

Dekker did so.

"And, Dekker, now that you know I'm not a liar, are you ready to cooperate and finally hear the truth?"

Dekker swallowed hard.

"Sit down, young man. I have words to speak to our friend through you. First, tell him that we greet him in the name of Baal. Tell him that we esteem him as a father. Tell him that he has come a long way from his own land to a land far to the north and a people not his own, but a people, nonetheless, who hold him in great esteem for his bravery and zeal, and who sympathize completely with his cause."

Dekker did all this. Translation was difficult and on one or two occasions he had to consult a lexicon.

"Tell him, the ancient history of the conflict between the house of Israel and Jezebel has been preserved, and it is well known, although most people think it a legend. There are only a few people on Earth who know the story is real and not all of them are friends."

There was no answer from the professor for an uncomfortable length of time. He simply gazed down at the tabletop.

Lord Ashworth sighed.

"This is going to be a long night. Tell him that with his help we will once and for all rid the world of . . . of his old enemy," continued Lord Ashworth.

"I beg your pardon," said Dekker. "I will say no such thing."

Lord Ashworth flicked a look at Dupree. Dupree smiled.

"Dekker, don't make me do something you'll regret," said Lord Ashworth. "We are at war with several nations, even if you do not know it. Do not meddle in things that are bigger than you. Do you understand me? This is why we need a patriot. You do love England I presume?" His tone and color rose as he spoke.

Dekker could see that this man was ready to do whatever it took to get cooperation. Dekker swallowed hard. "Who are these so-called enemies?"

Ashworth sneered at him, "You want me to tell you state secrets? You hardly qualify as trustworthy Dekker. No, I'm sorry. You just do as you are told."

Dekker knew he was in no position to argue. He turned to the professor and repeated the words Lord Ashworth had told him to say.

At first, the professor did not respond, but then slowly the old mouth opened into a rictus of sheer joy, and harsh laughter broke from the old throat.

"Could you not have chosen me a stronger body, Lord Ashworth?" it said in Babylonian.

Dekker translated, and Lord Ashworth chuckled.

"My dear Father," said Lord Ashworth, choosing his words carefully, "we work mostly in the dark. It is to you whom we must turn for illumination. Please allow me to explain where we are in our history, and soon you will see why it is so important that we have your knowledge. For you see, Father, that you alone possess the key to the Flame of Heaven."

There was a deathly silence in the room after this communication for the space of several heartbeats.

"How came you to this knowledge?" said the voice.

"The man you inhabit is a great scholar. It was only by chance that one of my own servants found him at work on the, er, tablets from your queen. These tablets together with the burner have only recently been found, and this find was made quite by chance. The allies of Israel have their soldiers roaming the land of Babylon even now. While they were searching the grounds with a magical eye that is able to penetrate the dirt, looking for chambers in which people may hide, they found the ancient vaults of the temple to Marduk. These documents were sent to scholars in Israel, who enlisted the help of the man you inhabit because of his ability to interpret Babylonian. Before we were able to gain control of the situation, the man you inhabit was able to communicate with the scholars from Israel. It comes as no surprise that we are being observed. Israel is ever watchful, for enemies surround her, but she does have powerful friends. That is why, my dear Father, we need the Fire."

A silence so intense followed that Dekker could hear every breath taken in the room.

"I must have more knowledge of the time in which I live," said the voice. "The enemy is subtle and powerful."

Lord Ashworth scowled. "Very well," he snapped, "but be warned that the agents of Israel are no doubt those who lurk outside. We do not have time to waste."

"How do I know you are not an agent of Israel yourself?" hissed the voice. "How can I tell you are not playing me for a fool?"

Lord Ashworth remained silent for a while, and then, without warning, uttered a great blasphemy against Heaven and all in it. These were exceedingly difficult words for Dekker to communicate, for even though he was not a Christian, he respected the faith of his wife. It was only after extremely violent threats against Kate that Dekker agreed to tell Obrahim what Ashworth had said.

The rasping laughter which broke from the old professor's throat was the only confirmation Ashworth needed of their mutual understanding and hatred. An almost comically wicked, hot grin broke over Ashworth's refined face.

"So, we have a common enemy, but that does not make me your friend," said the voice.

"True," said Ashworth. "I would give you my word, but surely, Father, you see your position. What choice have you? Come, work with us. Though we are powerful ourselves, we need you. Even if we possess the Fire, we do not know its power, and we will need instruction. We belong to a civilized people, where loyalty is richly rewarded."

The old head nodded. "The Flame of Heaven is a great weapon that cannot be resisted. Its destructive power is immense. While I was in prison I did not sleep, for the magic of Jezebel and the power of Baal has instructed me in its use."

Dekker spent the rest of an exhausting evening translating the questions from the professor's visitor about the modern age and its politics. A great deal of time was spent on ancient texts, many of which were available in the library. Some of these texts Dekker had never seen, and despite his extreme discomfort, he was impressed at the thorough forethought Ashworth seemed to have put into this encounter. Doctor Sikes seemed quite capable of finding his way around the library and seemed familiar with a great many of the texts. On one or two occasions, a call was put through to Sibyl for additional texts that might illuminate some point in history. No doubt she would arrive tomorrow from London with copies of the requested books or ancient manuscripts.

The voice seemed most eager to follow the progress of Babylon and Israel through history. Dekker was intrigued by how difficult this ancient priest found it to believe that the barbarian hordes to the north in Europe now had ascendancy in the world.

"And you are sons of barbarians?" said the priest in amazement.

Dekker relished putting these rank questions to Ashworth. The Lord bristled at the brazenness of some of the questions. This always raised a chuckle from the priest.

In the early hours of the morning, Dekker was made to relate Obrahim's story to Ashworth. Sikes had left at midnight. Only Dupree remained.

Ashworth looked at his watch. "Goodness, the time. No word from the sergeant?" He turned to Dupree, "Get hold of the sergeant and find out what's going on."

Dekker was impressed at the swiftness of Dupree's actions. A moment before, he had appeared to be in a light doze.

"Okay, Dekker, to bed with you. We have made good progress tonight, and well done. You know all that there is to know at this stage."

Dekker got up stiffly from the chair he had inhabited for the last five hours. Dekker was ravenously hungry, but too proud to ask Lord Ashworth for food.

The Flame of Heaven

"Before you go, Dekker, please bid our guest goodnight from me and ask him if his bed is to his satisfaction."

The voice did not answer immediately. Dekker tried again. "Lord Ashworth, we are in grave danger. We must leave immediately," said the harsh voice.

Chapter 14

Lord Ashworth hung up. Downstairs the sergeant punched one key on her cell phone.

"Yes, it's on. Do you have your men in place, and the dogs? We're going to have to smoke 'em out, no doubt. The road block . . . in place? Good. And be quiet about it, too. No sirens or lights, got it?"

The sergeant hung up, switched off the lamp beside her, and carefully pushed an inch of curtain back to stare out into the night. Nothing moved in the moonlight. She moved quickly through the house and knocked quietly on Kate's bedroom door.

"Come in," said Kate sleepily.

The sergeant pushed her head through the door and smiled at Kate.

"I'm afraid we have company. I'm going to have to lock you in now until morning."

"How is Dekker going to get into the room then?" Kate asked.

The sergeant looked her up and down. "Well now, honey, I guess Dekker will just have to sleep on the couch, won't he?" she said.

Kate did not answer; she merely looked at the sergeant steadily. The sergeant closed the door abruptly and locked it with some satisfaction. She removed the Glock from her holster and then hit the emergency cell number again.

"Yes, it's me again. This has to be done covertly, nothing gets to the ministry. We're probably dealing with Mossad, maybe a special services unit. By the way, have you found their vehicles yet? . . . No? Well, keep looking. They could not have teleported here."

A moment later: "In position? Good. I'll distract them from here. We have some high-powered security lights on the roof. If they're using night-vision, we'll temporarily blind them. Switch your night-vision off now," she ordered.

The sergeant took a remote control from her pocket. "Look away." She depressed several buttons. Outside, brilliant light lit the surrounding darkness. "Now, now, now! Rush them!"

Chapter 15

Lewis and Declan, ex-servicemen with the SAS, moved stealthily through the sparse stand of silver birch near the house. They squatted behind a straggling hawthorn bush. Declan removed night-vision binoculars from his jacket pocket and surveyed the house.

"Light on in an upper-story window, no movement, no guards, and no dogs that I can see. In fact, very suspicious," he said quietly to Lewis.

Declan glanced from his glasses to Lewis. Lewis was looking back over Declan's shoulder into the darkened woods, his face white as a sheet in the bright moonlight.

Declan spun around to see what had frightened Lewis. Neither of them was armed. They had spoken about this at length with Shelomo. Shelomo had said that if they got caught it would be because they had gotten careless, in which case it would be better not to be armed with military-style weapons so they could say they were birdwatchers who had become lost.

For just a split second, while turning to confront their enemy, Declan was sorry he had followed Shelomo's advice. If he was going to go down, he would prefer to do it in a fight. When he saw what confronted them, his resolve changed.

In a clearing among the trees stood a man, or more correctly the approximation of a man. The outline was humanoid, but the thing, whatever it was, had no features. Where its face should have been was a blank silvery oval. Draped from its shoulders was what looked like a long, linen garment of faintly luminescent silver. The linen rustled in the slight night breeze. It raised its hand in greeting. At the same time, several sensations invaded Lewis's and Declan's minds.

A voice, soft, liquid, and seemingly distant, but crystal clear said, "Peace be with you."

It took a step toward them. Both men felt the strangest sensation, as if they were off balance. It was only then that they realized the apparition, for you could not think of it as a man, seemed to be walking on air, about five centimeters or so above the ground and not quite plumb with the Earth's axis, as if it were in tune with another, truer axis.

"Aah, greetings," Lewis managed to stammer. Declan swallowed hard. Both men raised themselves from their squatting position and staggered to their feet.

"Who are you, sir?" Lewis managed to say.

For several heartbeats, the men confronted the blank face of the apparition of light.

"I am a fellow servant sent by the Most High."

Lewis and Declan looked down, not daring to gaze at the being before them and wrestling with an overwhelming desire to fall down and worship it, or run.

The apparition seemed to sense their disquiet. "Do not be afraid. Stay where you are. In a little while, I will bring you the captives you seek. You are to take them back to Shelomo. He will know what to do."

"Yes, sir," said Declan. Lewis nodded. Somehow they knew that the apparition smiled at them, though there was no change to the featureless oval.

"My brothers," it said, "when you take the captives back with you, as you exit the woods, you will find a group of men and two dogs standing in place, asleep. These men meant to harm you. They have what you humans call 'weapons' with them. You are not to disturb them, but simply walk past and go to your vehicle and then to Shelomo. Is that understood?"

"Yes, sir," they said in unison. Once again, that warm sense of friendship pervaded their minds. Then with rapidity that they could scarcely believe, the apparition made its way across the three hundred meters or so that separated it from the house. It stood on the porch just outside the front door.

Suddenly, the whole area was bathed in light. Three massive spotlights on the roof shone down onto the grounds surrounding the house. Lewis and Declan ducked for cover behind the hawthorn.

"Yikes! I think it might have set off an alarm," Declan whispered urgently.

"No," Lewis said thoughtfully. "No, mate. That light was meant for you and me. I think you and I had better be on our knees tonight and thank God. They were expecting us."

From behind their bush, the young men saw the angel take a step through the solid oak door and disappear slowly into the house.

Chapter 16

Kate heard a loud click as the lock mechanism turned in place. The door to her room swung open. She drew a frightened breath inward when she saw the luminous silver man. It took all of her willpower to stifle a scream.

"Do not be afraid."

She heard the crystalline voice in her head.

"Your prayers have been heard, child. The Father has sent me to take you to a safe place."

Joy thrilled through Kate's body. Could it be?

"My husband?" she stammered.

The angel lifted its hand and placed it before the lower third of its face as if to hush her. Then it beckoned her.

"Okay," mouthed Kate. She quickly pulled a pair of jeans on and then her shoes; she was still wearing her blouse and jumper for warmth. Then she cast her glance around for her bag.

The voice said, "No time. Follow me."

The angel moved through the gloom of the lower story of the manor toward the front door. As they reached the vestibule, they heard the tinny ring tone of a cell phone. Kate froze where she was.

"Yes, Dupree?" said the sergeant's voice.

As Kate's eyes adjusted to the gloom, she could actually see the sergeant standing next to the main window of the lounge room, looking out into the grounds through a crack in the curtains.

"We should have our intruders, or at least their warm bodies, in a couple of minutes. Stay up there for a little while and away from the windows. There may be stray bullets," she added and snapped her phone shut.

The angel stepped into the wall and disappeared from Kate's view. Just as it did so, the sergeant turned and saw Kate outlined by the moonlight filtering through the long vestibule windows. Kate could not think of what to do, so she smiled and waved in a friendly fashion.

"What the . . . who's that!" The sergeant flicked on the lamp she stood next to, and then moved away from the window, drawing her weapon as she did so in a fluid movement. A look of sheer incredulity swept over her features. Her eyes lit with fierce anger.

"How the hell did you get out of your room?" The sergeant leveled her weapon at Kate and walked toward her, taking careful steps. "And where the hell do you think you're going?"

"Sergeant, I wouldn't do that if I were you," Kate said evenly.

"Wouldn't you now? Well, I'll give you this much. You're a bold one."

As the sergeant walked through the entrance from the lounge into the vestibule, she sensed, more than saw, the angel's hand reach through the wall and seize her weapon. The weapon disappeared into the wall, and the angel stepped out. A look of unadulterated terror surged across the sergeant's features.

With a low moan, the sergeant collapsed in a heap at the feet of the angel.

"Is she—?"

"No, she lives. She sleeps."

"The gun?"

"It is inside the wall where this creature cannot go without tools," said the crystal voice. Then, "Wait here. I will try to bring your husband to you."

Kate shivered slightly as she watched the angel move down the passageway toward the far staircase. She heard the sound of muffled voices and the staccato of masculine laughter filter down the stairway. The phone on the sergeant's belt rang. Kate stepped toward the sergeant and then away, unsure of what to do.

                          ❦   ❦   ❦

Dupree lowered his cell phone from his ear. "She isn't answering." He looked across at Ashworth.

"I think we wait until she gives us the all clear," Ashworth said.

The professor cleared his throat. All three of the other men glanced in his direction. The professor faced the door to the study. The professor's gaze was transfixed on the doorway behind them. Something about the intensity of his gaze made the other men turn toward the door to see what he was staring at.

The angel stood before them in the room, the closed library door behind its shoulders.

"Good God!" Ashworth exclaimed and jumped about a meter back into the room, knocking into the professor and sending him reeling backward into the table.

Dupree drew his weapon with lightning speed. He leveled the gun, not at the angel, but at Dekker. The weapon spun out of Dupree's right hand before a shot could be fired, and Dupree fell to his knees evidently in great pain, holding his injured right hand with his still-functioning left hand.

Dekker stood rooted to the spot.

"Dekker will come with me," said the crystal voice, addressing the shelves about three paces to the left of the knot of men.

"What the . . . here you! Who do you think you are?" Ashworth said, waving his arms at the angel as if it were a half-wit.

A dry, cracked laughter issued from among the shelves.

Ashworth and the others now jumped about a meter to their right, sheer terror on their faces. From among the shelves, bright green smoke roiled and resolved itself into two feline eyes and a cracked-lipped mouth.

"He does not belong to you . . . all of these belong to me!" bellowed the mouth and knocked Ashworth, the professor, and Dupree into a heap of moaning bodies. Dekker was buffeted by the same wave of energy, but did not fall. A great dread threatened to overwhelm him and he staggered, holding his head in his hands.

The angel stood its ground and spoke to Dekker calmly, "If you give yourself to God, this evil one cannot harm you."

"Go, take the girl. These belong to me!" the mouth hissed. The face shot forward from the shelf toward Dekker. Dekker reeled backwards toward the door and the apparition. Both spirits terrified him. His mind was numb, unable to think clearly. All he wanted to do was run.

"He cannot harm you if you place your trust in Christ," said the crystal voice in his head.

"Go downstairs. You will find Kate at the front door. Head toward the trees directly in front of you. You will find two young men waiting for you. Go with them."

Dekker hesitated, his legs shaking beneath him.

"Go now," said the voice calmly. "I will try to protect you."

The angel took a step into the room and the green eye retreated. The eyes flicked in Dekker's direction, then toward the angel. Suddenly there was an almighty explosion of light. Coils of green light enveloped the angel. Out of the angel's mouth came a sound like a hammer blow, terrible and ferocious. The name of God filled Dekker's head. The other men held their hands over their ears and screamed. He felt a numb terror in every fiber of his being, but somehow his leaden limbs moved him toward the door.

The library door flew open and Dekker stumbled through; then finding reserves of courage, he sped down the stairs. He took a fleeting glance over his shoulder once he reached the bottom of the stairs. The angel was about three steps behind him, still facing the eyes and mouth, which had followed them down the stairs. Strange bursts of light flicked between the spirits and lit up the corridor, a phantasmagoria of color.

The mouth bellowed again, now in words or a language he did not understand and did not care to. Overwhelmed with dread, Dekker fell to the floor. On hands and knees he tried to scramble down the corridor. Kate was in his vision, her face a mask of terror.

"Run, Katie, run!" he screamed.

"No, no!" she wailed.

A gigantic burst of light issued from the mouth of the demon, followed by the most ferocious bellow Dekker had ever heard. It completely flattened him. He writhed on the floor, hands over his ears, but still his head felt like bursting.

Somehow the angel and the demon were between him and Katie now. He knew he was trapped. The angel stood between Katie and the grotesque face. Something that looked like a shield aflame hung on its arm and, incredibly, a sword the color of bright gold protruded from its mouth, toward the face. The green eyes flicked toward Dekker with an unmitigated hate fixed in their depths, malevolence so strong that Dekker knew that his own strength would fail him if he tried to resist.

"Kate, run! Run as fast as you can for the trees!"

"Dekker, no!" Katie cried.

"Run!" he shouted at her.

Their eyes locked as the two spiritual combatants faced off. Dekker got to his feet. The eyes inverted and peered back at him, then rushed toward him and smashed him to the ground. He lay still.

Katie's face was a mask of pain. Her eyes filled with tears.

"He lives. They will not kill him. They need him," said the voice in her head.

"Go now."

Katie turned and ran.

Dekker moaned and sat up looking to his right. Through a narrow window at the foot of the stairs he was gratified to see that Kate was already halfway across the expanse of lawn. Two white faces bobbed up behind the hawthorn bushes and beckoned her urgently. His head spun and his stomach heaved. He looked around him carefully. The eyes and mouth seemed to have disappeared. He scrambled to gain his feet and then felt a crushing weight on his back. A meter above his head hovered the malignant eyes and mouth.

"You are mine," it said.

"No, no!"

The eyes rushed toward him, furious hate in their depths. The blow was stunning and sent Dekker reeling down the corridor. The last thing he saw was the eyes peering down at him and then blessed darkness consumed him.

Chapter 17

"Who are you?" Kate said breathlessly. She stood behind the hawthorn bush catching her breath.

"Lewis, and this is Declan," said Lewis in a strong Scottish accent. "Look, Kate, I know this is hard, but . . ."

Kate held up her hand. "Don't worry. I believe you. The . . . angel. They have Dekker."

Gunshots rang out inside the house.

"Let's get out of here!" Declan said. "We'll explain everything in the car."

The three of them tore through the brush and into the stand of silver birches, more gunshots behind them. Katie prayed furiously that Dekker would be safe. Declan led, Lewis brought up the rear. Katie stumbled, between them, eyes streaming with tears. Suddenly Declan came to a halt, ducking for cover in the sparse trees. The others followed suit. In a gully between the road and the tree line stood ten men in dark combat gear and two German shepherd dogs. Bright moonlight glinted on the assault rifles slung across their shoulders. The night-vision goggles they donned made them look more like robots than men.

"Oh crap!" Declan said under his breath.

"The angel told us these blokes would be here . . . and asleep. I don't think we're in any danger. Just in case, I'll go first," he said and scrambled down the slope without further ado.

"Declan . . . no!" Lewis hissed, but too late. Declan walked down into the gully and approached the first soldier. The group of men stood inert. Declan waved his hand in front of the soldier's goggled face. The soldier did not move.

Declan turned with a grin on his boyish face and waved the others down. "Come on, let's go! No point in hanging around."

The three ran through the group of men, up the side of the gully, crossed the road, and loped about another two hundred meters to the right. A Land Rover had been unceremoniously driven into the thicket on the side of the road and hastily covered over. Now they uncovered the vehicle. Declan helped Katie into the back seat while Lewis fired up the engine. Just as they got into the Land Rover, a light rain began to fall.

"How convenient. That should cover our tracks in no time," Declan said. Katie watched nervously as Declan, who sat in the passenger's seat, drew a pistol from the glove box. "Just in case we have unwanted company," Declan said, smiling dangerously.

"Somehow I don't think we'll be needing that and just by the way, I thought we had agreed with Shelomo not to take weapons," Lewis said as he backed the vehicle carefully out of the thicket and onto the road. He revved the engine and took off at speed.

"Well, technically I did not have it on my person," said Declan in a thick brogue.

There was silence for minute as they sped down the highway.

"Oh no, Kate, get down! They were expecting us," Lewis said.

All three of them saw the flashing blue light on the side of the road and figures standing near a road barricade. Lewis slowed the Land Rover as the lights played over the figures and the hastily placed boom gate. He drew up alongside a police officer standing near the gate and rolled down his window.

"Evening officer," he said jovially.

The officer blinked, but said nothing. He simply stood in the rain staring into the middle distance.

"I think they've had the treatment too," whispered Declan loudly.

Lewis gave his brother a withering look.

"Um, officer would you mind if we went through. We're in a bit of a hurry," said Declan, leaning over.

The policeman blinked again.

"I think he's waking up slowly. Do me a favor Declan and open the boom gate will you," Lewis said quietly.

Kate sat with wide eyes in the back seat as Declan got out of the Land Rover, walked over to another police officer standing at the boom gate, waved his hand in front of the officer's eyes, shrugged his shoulders and then carefully lifted the boom. Lewis drove through and stopped momentarily to pick up Declan. They all looked at each other silently.

"Neat," said Declan.

Soon they turned from the road and were flying north along the highway. Declan turned and looked at Kate, "I'm sorry we were unable to get Dekker out," he said softly.

Kate smiled up at him and shook her head. "I don't think we had much choice. This thing is way bigger than all of us."

In the front seat, Lewis and Declan exchanged a quick glance.

Chapter 18

The sergeant recovered first. She found herself stretched out on the rug in the entrance of the manor. She sat up, rubbed her eyes, and squinted as she peered down the darkened corridor toward the stairway. She felt for her weapon.

Empty holster.

She staggered to her feet and bravely shuffled down the corridor, supporting herself along the wall with an outstretched arm. Further along, near the foot of the stairs, she found the inert Dekker. She bent over him and felt for a pulse in his neck—*still alive.* She listened intently. A muffled moaning sound emanated from the upper floor. The sergeant nudged Dekker in the ribs with her boot. Dekker moaned, his eyes opened, and he blinked.

"Get up," she said without emotion.

"Katie?" Dekker said.

"You had better pray that we can find her. Get up!"

Dekker struggled to his feet.

The sergeant steeled herself, taking three deep breaths; she ascended the stairs, pushing a groggy Dekker before her. A blaze of light spilled from the open library door into the darkened hallway. She and Dekker made their way carefully toward the light. Another moan—it sounded like Lord Ashworth. Dekker stumbled in and sat on the chair that had been lately vacated by the professor, holding his head in his hands, feeling ill.

The sergeant peered around the room. A shelf of books had collapsed, and books were strewn every which way across the floor. In among the debris was a tangle of limbs. She walked swiftly over to the tangle. She spied Dupree's weapon and put it in her own holster. Next, she knelt beside the moaning Lord Ashworth and slapped his cheeks hard. A satisfied look stole over her face as she did this.

His eyes fluttered open. "Ahhh . . . who?" Ashworth began.

"It's me, sir. What the hell happened up here?"

The sergeant helped Ashworth into a sitting position. He blinked heavily up at her as she squatted over him. His eyes moved across her face.

"Ahem, I hate to disturb you two, but we seem to have company again," Dekker said, an edge to his voice.

"There it is!" Ashworth pointed over the sergeant's shoulder, a look of sheer terror contorting his face.

Behind her, the sergeant heard what sounded like a sledgehammer smacking dirt and then a rain of fine sand on wood. She spun around, gun in hand. As soon as she saw the angelic apparition, she squeezed off three quick shots. The bullets passed through the angel's torso and smashed the window behind it. Dekker dove to the floor, not wanting to be caught in the crossfire. In the angel's hands were the fragments of tablets the professor had been studying.

"No!" Ashworth screamed. The sergeant ripped off another shot. Suddenly, the angel sped toward them. The sergeant let off a volley of shots at the speeding luminous figure.

With a flash of blue light, the angel passed through the far wall of the library and disappeared completely.

A deathly silence hung over the library. Then a low cackle of laughter broke the silence. The professor sat bolt upright and Dupree staggered to his feet moments later.

"What, what happened?" Ashworth stuttered. The wizened head of the professor turned a malignant gaze upon Ashworth. "I know where the Flame of Heaven is, you fool. Do as I say now and all will prosper."

For a moment, Lord Ashworth's eyes blazed hatred. Though he did not understand a word, the tone in which it was said was unmistakable. He struggled for self-possession. "What did he say?" snapped Ashworth. Dekker translated.

The sergeant swallowed down hard on a chuckle. The professor's bright eyes flicked from one face to the other.

He is a smart one; we'll have to be careful with him, she thought.

"Come, gentlemen," she said. "We are all in this together."

Both men turned to her.

"Quite," managed Lord Ashworth. "Since we are now friends," he said, turning back to the professor, "do tell, to whom am I addressing myself?"

"I am Obrahim, high priest of Baal and keeper of the Flame of Heaven."

Chapter 19

Lewis drove the Land Rover northwest into the Cotswold district. Soon they were on the back roads and then a narrower lane. They passed the village of Horsley, finally ending their journey in a cul-de-sac of sorts. They drove through a gate edged by a tall hedgerow. The dirt lane on which they traveled grew slick and rutted with puddled rainwater. They bounced their way along to a farmhouse that appeared through a copse of trees.

Katie looked at her watch; they had been traveling for about two hours. She was exhausted.

"We'll get some sleep soon," said Lewis, looking at her in the rear view mirror.

"Well, here we are, and a warm welcome to you." "Come along. We'll get some hot coffee and a rasher or two of bacon into you, and you'll feel good as new."

Katie managed a smile for her mysterious hosts. She and Dekker had been subject to such abuse over the last day or so that any kindness at all came as a pleasant surprise. Although they seemed much nicer and more trustworthy than Ashworth and his lot, Katie surmised, they were still strangers. This time she was not going to show her hand. She would keep quiet and keep her eyes open. She felt a fool for having been so easily gulled by Lord Ashworth and his henchmen.

"Lead on, McDuff," Katie invited. Lewis and Declan smiled.

"That's the spirit. You'll see soon enough that we mean you no harm," Declan said.

"I'll believe that when you put your guns away and I have my husband back," replied Kate.

"Fair enough, but the guns aren't meant for you," Declan said, his smile disappearing.

The sun rose over the eastern horizon just as they entered the farmhouse. To her very great surprise, the first person Katie saw as she entered the house was an attractive redheaded woman, who smiled at her in a friendly and sympathetic fashion. She had been expecting this to be a male-dominated situation, and she was secretly greatly relieved to have another female presence. The young woman walked forward shyly, her hand extended. "Hello Katie. Kirsten's my name. I work at the museum. We've managed to, well, I suppose infiltrate sounds like such a dirty word, but yes, we've managed to infiltrate the stronghold. I keep an eye on Sibyl Hardacre, the curator of the museum. She's deeply connected with this whole business too . . . but I'm going too fast."

"I must confess I'm puzzled," Kate said. "Plots, intrigues, infiltrations and this orb? What has all this to do with my husband and me and how do you know my name?"

"All good questions," said a deep voice behind them.

Katie turned. Behind them stood a man, not quite six feet tall with gray-flecked dark hair. His dark skin was smooth and hairless, his nose hawk-like, but his eyes captivated—bright dark pools that seemed to radiate intelligence, surrounded by a network of fine lines when he smiled.

"Kirsten, be a dear and put the kettle on, our guest must be famished," he said. The accent was strange. Flat vowels—like someone from the Middle East, or Eastern Europe—yet with the slightest Scottish lilt.

"Ay, this is our leader," said Lewis.

The man smiled at Lewis.

"Call me Shelomo, if you like," he said. "We will talk after you have breakfasted. We have important things to discuss."

Katie looked at Shelomo warily. "Who are you people? I'm not sure my husband and I want any involvement in this situation."

"We are the witnesses if you like. Witnesses to the last things."

Katie smiled a crooked smile, but Shelomo was not smiling now.

"So . . . what do you mean? You belong to a religious group of some description?"

"Do you honestly think this is all a coincidence, Katie?" Shelomo said.

"Well, no, not exactly."

Katie clasped her hands in front of her. Shelomo smiled again.

"Okay, but I'm not doing another thing until someone tells me exactly what's going on," Katie said firmly.

"That is wise, my friend, but the truth is that it is you who holds most of the information. But enough—all will be made clear soon enough. Let's eat," Shelomo said.

The smell of freshly cooked bacon and eggs filled the air, and Kirsten came forward with a tray full of steaming mugs of coffee.

For the first time in what felt like an age, Katie smiled a genuine smile.

The young men helped Kirsten prepare breakfast. The banter between the younger men and the older man was jovial but respectful. A quiet and gentle authority emanated from the man they called Shelomo. Perhaps it was the obvious respect that the other people in the room showed in subtle ways, but it felt almost impossible to be nervous or angry around him; or maybe it was just the fact that he was wearing Wellingtons and a raincoat and had obviously been doing something out in the yard. Kate gulped her first cup of coffee down, and despite herself ate a second helping of breakfast. Everyone ate heartily. Kirsten asked polite questions about Kate's past, where she grew up and how she had met Dekker. The mood grew somber again.

"Well, Kate. I'm sure you have questions. You are safe now. May I suggest you get some sleep and then you should be in a better position to make decisions?"

"So you mean I'm a prisoner again," said Kate quietly.

Shelomo looked at her with compassion.

"I'm sorry we weren't able to rescue Dekker. Here you're free to leave at any point."

Shelomo set a car key down in front of her.

"It's not much of a car. It's the old Toyota in the yard. But it will get you to London," he added, holding her gaze.

Silence fell over the group. Kate picked up the keys. She fought back tears.

"I'd be lying to you if I said you would be safe. They will be looking for you, Kate. For all of us."

Kate put down the keys again; this time tears brimmed in her eyes. Shelomo smiled. The young men move awkwardly in their chairs.

"Kate, you hold on to those keys," Kirsten said softly. "Only let me show you to your room and you have some sleep. If you need anything you give me a call, see. I'm just down the hall."

Kate nodded. "I won't need the keys," she said and smiled shyly up at Kirsten.

Chapter 20

Hassan Nasrallah, the supreme leader of Hezbollah, stared down into the crowd, his eyes searching and weary.

"Soon, soon the Zionist pigs will be routed. We will chase them into the sea!" he shouted.

The microphone gave off a hideous screech of feedback as the bloodthirsty crowd cheered their leader.

The Mossad secret agent, Jakob Meir, lifted his balled fist and chanted with the rest of the three-thousand-strong crowd. "God is Great," he screamed. He was always surprised to hear such vitriolic hatred come from the cherubic face of Nasrallah. Although only thirty years old, the Mossad agent was a seasoned veteran in the field. He remembered his first mission with Mossad in one of the Palestinian refugee camps in Lebanon. The shooting, the killing, the running, the fear of being found out; that was what he thought he would find most difficult, but no . . . this constant stream of hate talk about Israel was what he had found toughest to endure then and still did.

His eyes flicked through the crowd. Hezbollah would have their own agents working the crowds, looking for people like him. It was not uncommon to be invited to a quiet part of the stadium for an informal chat with the Hezbollah security. They usually worked the edges looking for signs of nervousness. Hate was a powerful intoxicant, and it was easy to spot someone resisting its effects, if you knew what you were looking for.

Jakob's eyes flicked to the left-hand side, searching the sea of faces. A white minivan with tinted windows had just pulled up very close to the crowd. A warning flared deep within his consciousness.

"Allah Akba," the crowd roared again as, above their heads, on a massive projection screen, they witnessed video footage of a bus exploding in downtown Jerusalem. That had been just last week. His fist went up automatically. "Allah Akba."

It occurred to him that the minivan itself would be an excellent suicide-bombing vehicle, *but surely not here in Baal Bek, the stronghold of Hezbollah. That would be a tactical blunder. He would have heard something through his contacts if Mossad were planning an event. Anyway, Israelis did not do suicide bombings,* he thought.

His eyes flicked to the right. On the far edge of the crowd, another white minivan had pulled up. Something was amiss. Another minivan nosed in behind it. He noted the positions of the minivan with the tinted windows to his left and two minivans on the slightly downhill slope to his right. Jakob turned in the crowd and started to make his way through the ranks of fanatics in their green headscarves, flying the green and white Hezbollah flags. The flags were good cover. He kept a weary eye on the balaclava-clad roughnecks at the edge of the crowd, assault rifles pointing to heaven, fingers on the trigger. He knew they would not hesitate to shoot anyone who was in the least suspicious.

"Where are you going in such a hurry, brother?" a voice said in Arabic.

"To take a piss, or should I just do it here, like a Zionist pig?" Jakob said in flawless Arabic, his dark eyes flashing a challenge.

The beardless man flashed him a smile. A smile of perfectly straight teeth, too perfect to be real.

"By all means, take a piss in the appropriate place, like a good Muslim."

The Flame of Heaven

Jakob lips curled into a sardonic smile as he shoved past. His eyes flicked right again; he clamped down hard on a feeling of panic. The lack of beard meant the man was no Hezbollah supporter. That made him nervous. That, together with the fact that no one had exited from the vehicles yet. That was surely a bad sign. The balaclava brigade seemed to have registered the minivans too. Three thousand supporters of Hezbollah crammed into the ancient temple of Apollo at Baal Bek would be an easy target for a suicide bomber— *but Jews do not commit suicide, especially religious Jews*, he continued to remind himself. *Or at least, not like this.*

Every instinct in his body told him to get out, run, and hide. He looked back at the stage. The Hezbollah leader spat more invective into the microphone to more cheers and ecstatic waving of the flags. The microphone gave off another ear-splitting screech. Jakob made his way more carefully toward the back of the crowd. He could no longer see the clean-shaven man he was speaking with a moment ago, and he lost sight of the minivans on the left side of the crowd as he passed behind the few broken pillars and bit of crumbled wall of the ruined temple.

Then what little doubt he had left in his mind left in a flood. His heart leapt in his chest. Nosing slowly toward him through the crowd was another white minivan with the same tinted windows, making its way directly into the ancient temple precinct.

Jakob glanced over his shoulder and looked up searchingly at Hassan Nasrallah on the stage. The man had his head to one side, talking to an aide, and pointing toward the minivan making its way into the heart of the crowd. Something was seriously amiss. Minivans, unless they were meant for some official purpose, would not be allowed into the temple precinct, even if it was an open precinct like this one. It was an ancient monument.

֎ ֎ ֎

Confused looks turned toward him in the sea of men as the minivan surged past Jakob. The crowd parted obediently, making way for the van. Jakob wanted to run as fast as he could, but controlled himself and moved quickly toward the back of the pulsing throng. The crowd fell in behind the minivan making its way slowly toward the stage, thinking it must hold someone important.

On the stage Nasrallah backed away from the microphone with a look of confusion on his face. Jakob saw the security detail talking rapidly into their headsets. Now assault rifles were coming off their shoulders. The balaclava toughs had leveled their rifles at the van and were gesticulating for them to stop. Jakob knew what was coming next. He pushed his way out of the press of bodies easily enough, now that everyone's attention was riveted to the minivan moving through the crowd. He moved rapidly toward the nearest solid structure, an outhouse toilet made from cement bricks, over the road from the temple. He gave one last look over his shoulder as pandemonium broke out. Nasrallah was literally being shoved off the stage by his security detail.

His heart leapt. *Could it be at last they had cornered the leader of Hezbollah?*

A man dressed from head to toe in black, including a face mask, leveled his assault rifle at the van and screamed into the microphone, "Stop the bus, or I shoot!"

A sudden surge rent the crowd of onlookers as fear descended like a vulture. People fell over trying to distance themselves from the bus. Jakob pulled his head back around the corner of the outhouse, sacrificing his view of the crowd for the security of the bricks. The staccato of an assault rifle echoed through the air. Then it happened. His heart turned to water in his chest as the familiar whump of high explosives rolled all before it. The ground below him shook vigorously. He lost his footing and slumped back against the outhouse wall. It was always the same. The distant echoes faded, and the terrible, terrible silence ensued for a moment or two after the initial blast, as minds too shocked to comprehend the carnage shut down.

The Flame of Heaven

Jakob allowed himself to slide down into a sitting position against the wall of the toilet block as the ghastly rain of twisted metal, dirt, stone, flesh and blood splattered down around him. His head sagged into his hands as he waited; he knew there would be another three explosions before it was safe to walk away. The screaming started. It occurred to Jakob in a blaze of surreal clarity that the most important aspect of his job was waiting.

High above the city center, a young man watched the pall of black smoke rise from the Temple of Baal Bek and listened to the distant screams of the dying. He smiled to himself and flipped open his phone.

"Yes, sir. It is done. Yes, the scrambler is on. The bombers did their work perfectly. The carnage massive . . . and I understand that Nasrallah is dead. Yes, sir, Dupree is down there and he reported to me moments ago that we have at least one Mossad agent in the crowd . . . Yes, sir. All electromagnetic frequencies are being monitored as we speak . . . Yes, sir. I realize the importance of this aspect." The Syrian nodded his head as he listened to the voice on the other side of the line.

"Yes sir, dead or alive, we will have a Mossad agent in custody soon."

Chapter 21

Lord Ashworth looked up from his desk as Harris Pinkerton, the secretary the International Criminal Court had provided his position, placed a thick wad of paper held together with a bull clip on his desk. The logo of the ICC graced its front cover.

"This is the report you said I should look out for Lord Ashworth," Harris said in his Midwestern drawl.

Ashworth looked up at his American secretary with what he hoped Harris would understand as withering contempt. Pinkerton's complexion, usually ruddy, was tinged with a little more red. Excitement sparkled in his eyes, and his short-cropped, sandy-colored hair and portly frame lent him an air of busyness and imminent apoplexy. Ashworth thought he might try to goad Pinkerton to apoplexy.

"What report?"

"The one you were expecting, sir . . . about the Hezbollah massacre and, um, Israel?"

Lord Ashworth gave him his hooded-eyed look. He had been most displeased that the machinery of the UN had placed this young man with him. Ashworth had done all in his power to have his own staffer appointed to the position of secretary and clerk of the Court, but apparently his efforts had been seen as somewhat outmoded. The UN bureaucracy provided staffers; it was the only way to ensure nepotism did not flourish. He had been warned in a crude way by the head of human resources not to rock the boat.

The Flame of Heaven

"I suppose you have read the report?"

"Yes sir, it is my job, sir."

"Please, please do me a favor and stop calling me sir. I'm not knighted, it's Lord Ashworth to you."

Pinkerton's face suffused with embarrassment, "Ah, yes . . . um, Lord Ashworth."

He handed the file to Ashworth.

Lord Ashworth stared at Pinkerton. "Well?"

"Would you like me to give you a summary, Lord?"

"I hope that is not sarcasm Pinkerton, I'll have you flogged."

"I beg your pardon, sir but . . ."

"Oh, do please spare me your high dudgeon. You know you Americans lack humor. Do get on with it Pinkerton. Pray tell, I'm all ears."

Pinkerton looked at Lord Ashworth coolly, then said: "This report holds evidence of Israeli complicity in this brutal massacre of Hezbollah supporters and their leader at Baal Bek."

"I see, go on," said Ashworth. He could feel a smile creeping over his face.

"They managed to capture a Mossad agent, one Jakob Meir."

"And who is this 'they' you refer to?"

"The Lebanese police, sir. Apparently the great grandson of Golda Meir. Quite coincidental how they caught him really. Apparently someone saw him walking away after the fourth explosion, calm as you like. He walked into town and made a phone call from a call box on the street. It is routine for the public phones in Lebanon to be bugged. You would have expected that a Mossad agent would know that . . . anyhow."

"Such an ugly word, Pinkerton, that word bugged—do go on."

Pinkerton much to his own chagrin, flushed scarlet. For some odd reason he really cared about what this man thought of him— this was the sort of man who could make or break a career at the UN.

"Uh, yes Lord Ashworth, well they had a fix on the time and location, and were able to decipher the call. Apparently, he made the call directly to the Mossad headquarters, detailing the massacre and wanting to know what to do next. He is in custody and does not deny being a Mossad agent. The Israeli government of course is denying any complicity."

"Hard to believe, given their agent was right there. And, of course, the motive would be the Jerusalem bus bombing, what, a week ago?"

"Well sir, there is a complication. Some members of Hamas are taking credit for that bus bombing, and Hezbollah are denying that they targeted that bus. It is well known that Hezbollah usually go after hard targets . . . military targets."

"So, are you saying that Israel got it wrong, that their extra-judicial murder of the head of Hezbollah was a mistake?" said Lord Ashworth.

Pinkerton hesitated. He looked into Ashworth's eyes. They reminded him of a snake's eyes. He knew he was this man's stooge—*better not to rock the boat,* he thought.

"It would appear so, sir . . . Lord."

Pinkerton continued, "Hezbollah are bringing a charge of human rights violations against Israel in the International Court and call this an act of war. The Syrians are backing them. Their government is saying that the Hezbollah rally was a peaceful demonstration against Israeli aggression. Of course, while Hezbollah are denying any complicity in the Jerusalem bus bombing, to their disadvantage is the fact that they were showing a film of that bus bombing when the suicide mission ensued against the Hezbollah leader."

"Mmm," said Lord Ashworth thoughtfully.

"There is one more complication."

"And what might that be?"

"The suiciders, to a man, appear to have been Christian Lebanese militants, Lord Ashworth."

"Interesting, but hardly surprising Pinkerton. Mossad do not commit suicide. They would get someone to do their dirty work for them."

"Well, sir, that's just the thing," said Pinkerton, getting excited and forgetting himself. "The Christian-dominated Lebanese government is saying that the Baal Bek bombing is nothing more than a Syrian pretext for war. They say they had nothing to do with it."

Lord Ashworth looked up quickly into the eyes of his secretary.

"What do they base that allegation upon? Do they have evidence?"

"Well, it is unclear who intercepted the call that Jakob Meir made. The Lebanese are not saying how they came to find out about Jakob Meir, but, of course, their secret service is riddled with Syrian informants. The government is saying that the transcript of the conversation—it's in the file by the way—makes it clear that Jakob Meir was not reporting having undertaken the bombing; he was simply reporting the bombing."

Lord Ashworth's expression soured.

"I'll have a look at the transcript myself. In the meantime, please prepare this for trial."

The secretary looked at Lord Ashworth with a stunned expression.

"Begging your pardon, Lordship, but should we not look at the strength of the evidence first? This incident could easily precipitate a war between Syria and Israel."

A look of cold fury swept through Lord Ashworth's eyes.

"Mr. Pinkerton," Lord Ashworth said in a low voice, "you are my secretary, and you will do as I say. You must not think that these reports are the only channel of information I have at my disposal. I have it on good authority that this is the first of many atrocities that Israel plans to commit in order to foment war with her neighbors. My efforts in this court are to try to foment peace, not war, Mr. Pinkerton. A charge of human rights violations may bring Israel to her senses before she commits any more of the outrages I have been informed will take place within the next month. I too approach all such information with skepticism, but the fact that information I had at hand has just now been confirmed suggests some mischief."

"Yes, sir but there is just one more thing I'd like to point out, sir. This was a suicide mission and frankly Jews do not do suicide missions, sir. They have never in their history, nor have they ever paid anyone to do it, sir. It's quite true that Christian Lebanese have from time to time, but then we would have to establish a connection and that would be the first of its ki . . ."

"Mr. Pinkerton!"

"Sir?"

"Lord Ashworth to you, Mr. Pinkerton, and frankly Israel is quite capable of changing their tactics. Has it ever occurred to you that there are Palestinians who actually side with Israel? If even they would then why not Lebanese Christians? Consider the prize. Hassan Nasrallah himself. Do you honestly think the Lebanese Christian faction would do something like this themselves? They wouldn't dare. No one wants another civil war in Lebanon."

Pinkerton was flustered, but pressed on.

"Lord Ashworth, with all due respect, that's the point I'm making. This does not make sense, sir. We could be looking at a third force. Maybe there was a falling out between Nasrallah and the Syrians?"

"My dear Mr. Pinkerton, you need look no further than Israel as the third force . . . Occam's razor and all that," Ashworth said, a smile twitching across his lips as he finished his sentence.

Mr. Pinkerton looked away from Lord Ashworth, unable to hold eye contact.

"Theory, Mr. Pinkerton," said Ashworth through a sneer.

"Yes, sir. I was simply basing my advice on the information I have at my disposal. I shall prepare the court papers."

Lord Ashworth remained silent, simply staring at Mr. Pinkerton.

"Is there anything more, your Lordship?" No answer. "Then I'll go," said Pinkerton miserably. He had hoped his sleuthing would impress Lord Ashworth, but it seemed to have had the opposite effect.

"No . . . wait; actually there is one more thing, Mr. Pinkerton. I hope that you are not secretly a Zionist sympathizer? That will simply not do. In the ICC, we must take a strictly neutral stance on such issues."

Mr. Pinkerton blushed. "Well I—I do hold a neutral view on the issues of Zionism, sir . . . Is there anything else, your Lordship? Then I'll go."

Mr. Pinkerton turned slowly and walked out of the room. He could feel Ashworth's eyes boring into his shoulder blades.

The door closed. Lord Ashworth scowled to himself for a moment and then picked up the phone, punched in a number.

"Dupree, do me a favor. Put a tail on Pinkerton . . . yes, my secretary. I'm not sure the man is trustworthy. I think he may be harboring some, shall we say, unfashionable views. I want to know who he meets with and what he says for the next week or two. Got it? Good." Ashworth hesitated for a second, "Oh, by the way, how are the preparations going for our trip to Babylon? Excellent, and remember the team of archaeologists and diggers should be local. No Jews and for God's sake, no Christians if you can help it. I want no slip-ups. This has to go off without a hitch. The plan is in motion, and the timeframes are tight now."

Lord Ashworth listened intently for a moment, and then snorted to himself, "I see. Our priest is a womanizer then. Well, I don't suppose that is out of character for a priest. Frankly, I care nothing for his appetites, but make sure that he does not pass on information. He must be kept under surveillance at all times. He is our only link to the . . . er, object. As to Dekker, why don't you see if you can get him interested in a woman? Yes, I know you understand. That will strengthen our persuasiveness with him. He does worry me a bit. Yes, I know you have him under control. Good bye."

Ashworth put down the phone and swung his chair around to face the window. Outside was The Hague. The sky was suffused in a pinkish glow; winter was drawing to an end. The promise of spring had arrived with the first sprouting of the poplar leaves along Carnegieplein. He had noted that only this morning.

His breath caught at the back of his throat, he spluttered, then swallowed hard. To his surprise he heard himself sob. A feeling he had not had since he was a young man welled up inside him; a feeling of unfathomable longing, deep and vast, shot through with the most powerful sense of regret. A longing for—he knew not what. A sudden tear trickled down his smooth face.

"For god's sake, Ashworth. Get a grip," he muttered to himself.

Ashworth swung his swivel chair violently away from the view of the coming Spring . . . it had a way of reminding him of her—Tara—his late wife . . . before that cold hand had gripped his heart and mind. How had it happened, how? His eyes lifted to a beautifully framed full-color photograph of Bath Abbey hanging on the wall opposite. A gift from his wife. The place they had been married.

Without warning the glass covering the photograph cracked, and then the whole picture fell with a great clatter to the floor.

A rush of terror invaded his mind. A stifled choke wrung from his throat. His face, a violent tinge of red. Now he remembered. The giant cold fist clenched around his heart and a searing pain shot down his left arm. Now he remembered the day, the moment he had swapped the power of love, for the love of power. The tear which had trickled down his face left a dry track as the gloaming faded to black. Ashworth stared into the dark, numbed to the very core of his being as Fury uncoiled within him, seethed through him, searching out any feelings of light or sympathy. He could feel Fury, cold, hard, merciless, Traitor! Traitor! screeched Fury in his mind—putting all before him to death. Making all the small Ashworths within him bow, every memory and every feeling, a captive. He tried to plead and then to struggle, but could not move; not even a finger, as the relentless search continued.

"Worship Fury! Bow down to Fury!" bellowed the beast within.

Chapter 22

"Marook! Marook!" Shelomo called over the ambient clatter of copper and bronze smithing ringing in the afternoon air.

"Yes my friend," said a gravely voice from behind a shining column of copper pots.

Shelomo squinted into the dark of the shop interior. Marook stood quietly in his sooty workman's toga, his broad shoulders and rough hands, Shelomo knew, hid a gentle spirit. One of his massive hands rested on the shoulder of a shy-looking boy.

"Marook, things have come to a head and I'm sure that Shumash has sent spies to follow me here. I have brought trouble to this house today."

Marook glanced down at the sword worn loosely at the scribe's side.

"Be at peace. Yeshua, go and bring some of the hot herb for our guest."

"Yes, Father," said the boy and sped off.

Shelomo sighed and cast a nervous glance over his shoulder, then turned back and said, "Does Yeshua know where it is?"

Marook smiled and nodded. "Obrahim was devious and very distrustful, but he does not know his way around Babylon. After your message, we got him to relax. That priest drank a great quantity of my tea as he waited for Barook to fashion a replica of his precious orb. He would not let Barook touch it,

The Flame of Heaven

only look at it while he fashioned the replica. He insisted that he wanted to keep the original in sight at all times and refused to leave despite my assurances. I made sure that he did not see Yeshua in the shop and when he left, as you suggested to me, Yeshua did indeed follow him at a safe distance."

Shelomo looked at Marook with fondness, "Where is your oldest son? You must thank him for me, and of course Yeshua too. It would have been a dangerous and courageous action to follow that priest. Thank you Marook, this is more important than you know." Shelomo took a bag of silver and put it on the tray to his left. "That is for your troubles and your courage, it is the least . . ."

"No, no my friend. What are you doing? We will not accept this payment. We are friends."

"Please Marook. Where I am going I will have no need of this. For all the years of faithful service . . ."

"No. What do you mean . . . where are you going? Are you leaving Babylon?"

Shelomo smiled and grabbed the burly man by the shoulder and gave him a hug.

"Marook, these are dangerous times . . . please. There is no guarantee that Shumash will leave you be when I go. In fact, he will not. I have a tail. The eunuch Kashka and his perverts are following me. He is many things that eunuch, but a subtle man he is not."

Marook was silent for a few moments, then, "That is a great quantity of silver Shelomo? Where did it all come from?"

"It is the fair price for faithful service done for the temple and me over the years," said Shelomo.

There was an uneasy silence between the men. The boy, Yeshua, came back with a tray and a steaming long-necked copper pot. The tray clattered loudly on the stone-topped bench.

"Marook—no it is not like that. I did not steal from the treasury. This is my money . . ."

"You must be a very wealthy man, Shelomo," Marook said doubtfully.

Shelomo looked into Marook's eyes, this time without a smile.

"I have been around for a long time. There are many things you do not know about me— and that is for your own good, my friend. I have always been honest with you. Yes, I am a wealthy man, a very wealthy man."

Suddenly Marook shuddered. Despite his great size, his face looked pinched. Shelomo realized he was scared. Slowly Marook reached out and picked up the silver.

"Are you one of them—an ancient one?" Marook said softly.

Shelomo held his eye, then nodded slowly.

Marook stood, too terrified to look up. "I have had my secret thoughts about you Shelomo," he said with a quaver in his voice.

"Do not be afraid, Marook, I am flesh and blood, just like you. It is the Lord who has touched my life. It is Him you should fear, not me. I have spoken of Yahweh before. I am merely His servant."

Marook looked up, his eyes bright, but said nothing.

"If I were you, I would take your wife and sons and daughters on a long journey. You are Assyrians, no? Do you not have family in Nineveh?"

Marook nodded.

"Go to Nineveh and trade there for a time. All this will pass soon."

"I will do that," said Marook. Yeshua looked up at his father and smiled. Marook looked down and smiled uneasily at the boy.

"Come, we must hurry. There is little time left. Instruct your wife to pack the camels. Tell Barook to come with us and bring a sword. We may have some fighting to do before the day is out."

Shelomo knelt on eye level with the boy. "Yeshua, you have been a brave and clever boy, now tell me, where did that man hide the orb?"

"Tell him," said Marook, "Tell the man. I must go and speak with your mother and sisters."

"He went to the Temple of Gula for a bath and massage. While he was in there he threw it into one of the latrines on the west side of the temple when he thought no one was looking," said the boy simply.

"What! Are you sure, Yeshua?"

Yeshua smiled and said, "Yes, sir, I am. When he went into the temple I climbed the latticework on the outside. You can see into the bathhouse and the temple from there. I did not have a shekel to give to Gula so I could not enter. The man sat on the latrines there until no one else shared the room and then he quickly dropped the incense burner into the latrine next to him. I feel sorry for the person who is made to retrieve it," the boy said with a grin.

Shelomo smiled despite himself and mussed the boy's hair.

"Did he see you looking through the lattice?"

"I do not think so. He did not have much time to look around because some more men came in soon after that. Then he got up and went into the bathhouse."

"Do you think you can show me which latrine he dropped it into?"

"Yes, sir, it was the very last one to the right," said the boy brightly.

"Good boy."

Marook and Barook came back holding short swords. The young man's eyes were bright and a dangerous smile completed the picture.

"Steady Barook. We will only use the swords if our own lives are threatened. For now hide the swords under your togas. We will need some rope too, Marook," said Shelomo.

The older man nodded and indicated a coil of rope lying in the corner.

"Barook, you will listen to me and only do as I do," said Marook in his bass voice. He lifted his toga and fastened the sword around his waist, then he took the coil of rope and

Barook helped him wrap it around his chest and waist. Finally he replaced his toga. He was a big man and the extra bulk under his clothing did not look out of place. Barook nodded solemnly and fastened his sword underneath his toga.

"Yeshua, if there is trouble I want you to run back home and get your mother and sisters onto the camels, do you understand?"

"Yes, Father," said the boy, his eyes wide with unease as he eyed the sword and caught some of the solemnity of the grownups.

Shelomo smiled down at him as he hid his own sword, then patted his head again. "You have been brave, Yeshua, now lead us. There is nothing to fear."

At this the boy brightened again.

"Let us go out the back way," said Marook. "There is a man in a blue turban that has been outside feigning interest in pots since you arrived, Shelomo."

Chapter 23

Kate looked out of the window as the airplane rose steeply above the Bosphorus. Down below was Istanbul, and the next stop would be Jerusalem. Kate hoped that their tactic of taking staggered flights and not traveling directly to Baghdad would work. Air travel made her feel uneasy. She put her hand on the side of the airplane fuselage and felt the steady vibration. If Dekker had been there, she knew her hand would be in his.

Declan, two seats away, gave her a quick smile. She could not see his eyes through the dark glasses. Kate smiled back and glanced up and a few rows along. Lewis was seated quietly, near the jump seat on the far side of economy class. She could just make out the top of his head. Shelomo and Kirsten had gone on ahead of them. They would all meet in Jerusalem and then travel to Baghdad across country. She sighed. It was only a four-hour flight to Jerusalem, but she was nervous. She thought about the hajibs she and Kirsten had purchased in the markets in London. That had been fun, among the tinkling trinkets and flashing smiles of the salesmen, but always tinged with a little nervousness, as behind them, either Declan or Lewis or both of them would wander around like tourists, but alert for trouble. Always her mind wandered back to Dekker and then every bit of joy or peace would disappear. Kirsten assured her that they could not risk harming him, because they needed his language skills.

At the farmhouse they, as a group, had considered another rescue operation, and they had prayed, but in the end Shelomo said that trying to rescue Dekker now would be too risky and might even put his life in jeopardy, not to mention theirs. The situation was as it should be, however painful that was. Kirsten went back to work and was responsible for booking the flights for Lord Ashworth and Dupree to Baghdad in early spring; she resigned soon afterwards. Sybil Hardacre did not seem heartbroken when she left. Shelomo was delighted with this intelligence Kirsten was able to give about their flights. Kate smiled as she remembered how Kirsten had blushed when Shelomo had kissed her on both her cheeks and Declan and Lewis ribbed her mercilessly. Kirsten was proud of her work.

Through those weeks Kate often found herself daydreaming about how life worked out. Just months ago, she and Dekker led a quiet if somewhat unexciting life in their little flat in Bloomingdale. Now their lives had been turned upside down and filled with intrigue and fear. Shelomo and the others were all nice and friendly she thought to herself, but they were also very focused people and members of some sort of ancient secret order.

If she had understood correctly, they had been around for a long, long time: thousands of years, or more. Could that really be? Their questions were mainly aimed at what Dekker had told her, which was not much . . . mostly information about Professor Whitely and what the presence in him had said and questions about the cuneiform tablets, which Dekker had only seen very briefly. Kate remembered the look on Shelomo's face. He seemed shocked, almost scared and that had scared her more than she cared to think about.

"Then, it is time," he'd said.

"Time for what?" said Kate.

"Time for action. Dekker has done well. I know what they're looking for and I know where it is," said Shelomo.

"Where what is?"

Shelomo had smiled that slow smile. "The Flame of Heaven is what they are looking for."

"What is this 'The Flame of Heaven'—is it some sort of occult treasure or something? That's what Dekker said to me . . . some sort of occult object," said Kate.

Shelomo had given her a quizzical look. "I suppose you could call it that. Certainly, that is what its owners meant it to be used for. But God is the sovereign ruler and he may use anything for the good."

The conversation that followed had left Kate confused and even more scared. In her presence there was a long conversation between the people in the room about very ancient history and things too fantastic to believe. She sat silently, just listening while the others asked Shelomo questions and he answered methodically and without any dramatics. Certainly if they had not gone through the terror they had just endured, she thought, even she would never have believed what Shelomo said. She knew Dekker would have thought it insane. Kate looked at the others in the room. All of them sat quietly, absorbed in what Shelomo was saying.

"What I don't understand is why Dekker and I have to be involved at all. If you know where this damned object is, why didn't you just go and get it?"

Shelomo looked down for several moments, smiling thinly. Finally he said, "It is a question that I have asked many times. Why don't I just go and get the object and destroy it? The answer has been a firm 'no'. And there is wisdom in this. Firstly, it is a dangerous object. It is full of the wrath of God. Secondly, it is safe where it is. Third, to unearth it would take a team of excavators and the country in which it is located has not been amenable to western teams of excavators for some time. Finally, but this is just my thought on the subject, the unearthing of this object is like God's last act of mercy to his enemies. It is as if He is saying to them, you have unearthed this, you know what it is for, and therefore you are responsible for the consequence that it brings."

"And what consequence would that be?" said Kate, impatience etching her voice.

"Judgment, Kate," was the short reply.

Kate swallowed hard as she remembered that last statement. As for Shelomo— well, he was a gentleman but he was just plain unnerving, really. She had tried not to be in his company alone at the farmhouse. How old he was, he would not say. Kate smiled to herself again as she remembered her blunt questions. Maybe there had been wisdom in Shelomo's refusal to answer questions about himself. She had tried to talk to Kirsten about Shelomo, but it was quite clear after several aborted conversations that she was not going to say too much either. She just smiled and shook her head. Everyone connected to Shelomo had come from a family long associated with him and there seemed to be a sort of inbred reticence on the subject, much like true believers everywhere these days. The subject was so otherworldly that it was difficult to explain to anybody without them thinking you a fool.

Kate put her head to the side on a small pillow wedged between the fuselage and the seat and tried to sleep.

She woke with a start, surprised that she had fallen asleep despite her nerves. The captain of the El Al flight announced their descent into Jerusalem. The flight seemed to have taken only moments.

The checkout at Jerusalem went smoothly. They met up with Shelomo and Kirsten at the airport and Kate was genuinely happy to see them again.

As they walked through the terminal Kirsten said, "I made the reservation as close to the Dome as possible. With a bit of luck we'll be able to fit in some sightseeing." None of the men said anything. Kirsten added, "Lewis, be a dear and collect the car for us, please." Kirsten explained where she had parked the car.

Lewis smiled. "But of course, my dear," he said with mock irony. No one was fooled. He and Kirsten seemed to have grown close during the winter.

Minutes later Lewis waved from the window of a Land Rover. Declan strode about three meters behind the group— *still taking precautions*. As they walked toward the SUV a cell phone rang. Kate was surprised to see Shelomo dig into his

The Flame of Heaven

pocket, greet the caller shortly in a foreign language and then listen intently—*was someone expecting them? This was becoming even spookier,* she thought. *How many people were involved?*

The baggage was stowed and they all bundled into the SUV. Declan drove. Lewis opened the glove box and extracted an automatic pistol.

"Is the clip full?" Declan asked Lewis. Lewis checked the clip and breech of the pistol expertly, then he looked up into the rear view mirror and smiled. "How is everyone?"

Kate smiled back. "Well enough, but honestly is that gun really necessary, and how is it that we even have one in our possession?"

Declan nodded slowly. "Well, we have contacts here."

There was silence for a time while they navigated the thick rush-hour traffic.

"There is some bad news," Shelomo said suddenly.

All waited expectantly. "The bad news is that Ashworth is in town. He's investigating some incident. The leader of Hezbollah was assassinated and they have captured some Israeli spy, Jakob Meir. It turns out Jakob is the great, great grandson of Golda Meir, one of the past prime ministers of Israel. Jakob is kicking his heels in a Lebanese jail, possibly being tried for crimes against humanity, and you will never believe who the presiding judge is? Ashworth is in town speaking with the Israeli government about the incident before it goes to trial. Naturally tensions between Lebanon and Israel are high. The Lebanese are accusing the Israelis of assassinating Nazrallah. Israel denies any involvement and is demanding their agent's return. In the meantime Israel is accusing Syria of fomenting war, because Israel knocked out their nuclear program with an air strike about two years ago . . . if you remember. All very complicated. The long and short of it is that this will lead to some complications. I'm going to try to move our schedule forward a bit."

Declan looked up into the rear view mirror again.

Kate looked thoughtful, then said, "Well how does this really affect us? I mean we were expecting them in Baghdad about now, so another few days ducking and weaving trying not to get spotted is irritating, but not awfully bad? Besides they might have Dekker with them," the last bit in a hopeful tone.

Shelomo shrugged his shoulders. "I don't know, you could call it a hunch, if you like, a prompting. Things are drawing to a close and we need to move fast. The upshot for us is that Ashworth will probably have Dupree and his henchmen with him . . . there is little doubt about that. So we need to be on our guard. There is definitely something more going on that I haven't foreseen. We will only be here a day or two now to get everything ready for our trek across Jordan, but between now and then we must remain vigilant. Things are very tense in Jerusalem and there is an intifada on because of the assassination of Hassan Nasrallah. They're blaming Mossad, so avoid public transport!"

Chapter 24

"The body?" said Dupree in Arabic. His dark eyes scanned Gal'ed Street over the roof of the mustard Peugeot 304. His eyes dropped and met the fierce gaze of the Hezbollah commando in the halogen glow of a distant streetlight.

"In the boot. He was walking his dog, like you said he would be. Faisal got a body shot. Then we put him into Israeli commando fatigues."

Dupree's unfriendly gaze hardened even further. He waited a moment or two then said, "Aren't you forgetting something?"

"What? We did like you said," said the Hezbollah man.

"The bloody dog. I hope you did not let him get away?"

The young man's face pinched slightly. And his eyes wavered momentarily.

"You let the dog get away? Where do you think the dog will go . . . that's right, you young fool. Straight back home and then Ariel Zimmerman's wife will know that something is wrong with her husband!" spat Dupree.

A moment passed. The young man's face bunched into a snarl, but he said nothing.

"Okay, okay. We can fix this. Just don't mess up again. Send one of your men back to kill Mrs. Zimmerman and the bloody dog and get rid of the bodies." Dupree ducked down further to make eye contact with the men in the back of the car. "The rest of you get ready, we're about to liberate Palestine."

Chapter 25

Marook, his two sons, and Shelomo left the shop by the back door. Shelomo glanced left, down the street: women and children, hurrying home, the streets and alleyways emptying. *Quite a bit of activity, a good time to move,* he thought to himself. The scattered shards of the afternoon sun collecting at the upper stories of the buildings. Long shadows made it impossible to see faces distinctly.

"You three go first, as if you are going for an afternoon stroll. I will follow."

Shelomo stepped out of the shop's doorway and followed the three figures at a distance. The ziggurat loomed massively before them, its upper reaches towering over the sprawl of houses. Smoke rose from the altar on its summit to the god Marduk.

They moved down the narrow street smartly and then onto a main road. At a shop front selling fine pottery, Shelomo slowed as if interested in the wares. He ducked quickly under the linen awning and looked back into the hazy afternoon sun, to his left again—no familiar faces, or turbans. Nothing seemed out of the ordinary. Yet somehow the feeling that they were being watched grew with every step.

"May I help you, sir?" the voice broke into his thoughts.

"Uh, oh. No thank you. I was just thinking of a present for a friend, but not tonight."

The shop owner looked at him through bushy eyebrows and smiled through his grizzled beard, then winked.

The Flame of Heaven

"Something for a young lady, sir?"

The shopkeeper looked into the eyes of the man and could see that he had made the wrong assumption.

"Your daughter? . . ."

Shelomo stepped away and walked rapidly now toward the Ziggurat. The crowds were thinning and the smell of wood smoke and coal wafted through the air; soon the street he walked down was hazy with smoke that signaled suppertime.

The haze lifted as he entered the square surrounding the ziggurat. In the far left corner, now cast in the shadow of the mighty temple complex, stood the much smaller shrine to the dog god, Gula, the god of health. A cooling breeze blew up from the Euphrates River. Marook and his sons slowed and were casting glances over their shoulder as they neared the shrine. Yeshua waved at him as he recognized Shelomo, only to have his older brother grab his hand and say something sharply to him. Shelomo could not help smiling.

As he drew near to them a troop of four youths burst from the shrine, laughing uproariously. Shelomo watched them carefully—no danger, just foolish, exuberant youth. No doubt having made their oblations to the god, and having a bit of fun with the temple prostitutes, they thought they were ready for more sin.

Marook and his boys walked into the shrine complex. Shelomo loitered outside. The solitary eunuch on duty at the entrance to the shrine was nowhere to be seen. To the left was the room in which patrons disrobed, with the latticework high upon the wall to let in daylight. Shelomo smiled to himself again. It was fortunate that Marook had sent Yeshua to follow Obrahim. Only a child could have climbed the latticework without invoking suspicion. He had been in the service of the great God Yahweh long enough to know that these things were not fortunate coincidences.

Although the sun had not quite set, the shrine's disrobing room was dark.

A candle or sconce should've been burning in the disrobing room by this time, thought Shelomo.

The first faint stirring that all was not right stole through Shelomo's mind.

He drew up in front of the entrance and glanced back as casually as he could across the square. To his right was a gaggle of chattering women with water pots balanced on their heads, filling them at the neighborhood well in the cool of the day. Wells like this one dotted the banks of the Euphrates, which ran though the center of the city.

A man wearing a red turban exited the shrine, almost bumping into Shelomo as he looked back suspiciously at Marook and his sons loitering near the entrance to the disrobing room. Shelomo gave one more quick glance into the darkening shadows on the other side of the square. He could see movement, but no recognizable figures.

Within the shrine's precincts, the light was dimmer still, just enough light to make your way carefully. A statue of the dog god stood on the far side of a sunken rectangular room. Under its gaze burnt votive candles and bowls of incense smoldered their heady odor into the air. Between the god and Shelomo was a stone-carved latticework. Sconces were burning in the bathhouse at the foot of the god and faint murmurings of attendants and devotees receiving their wash; but to the right the disrobing room and the stairwell that led into the bathhouse was in darkness.

Shelomo stepped into the disrobing room and stopped for a moment to let his eyes adjust to the gloom.

Marook and his sons were at the far right corner of the room where a semicircle of latrines were situated.

"Down here, Father. This is the one," whispered Yeshua in his clear soprano voice. Shelomo took a step forward toward the trio, smiling to himself. *Almost too easy,* he thought.

"Oh, Shelomooo . . . Shelomoo!" another soprano voice called from outside, carrying clearly on the night air through the latticework above their heads.

The four figures inside the change room froze for a moment. Shelomo indicated with an agitated wave of his hand that Marook and Barook should take up positions on either side of the door.

"What! You, Kashka? Can a man not take a crap in peace!"

A girlish giggle wafted in from the gloaming outside.

"I have soooldiers with me Shelomo, don't make me send them in to come and get you," said the singsong voice of the eunuch.

"Are you threatening me?" replied Shelomo, managing to sound annoyed and confused at the same time.

"Where're your friends, are they with you?"

Shelomo looked into the fierce visage of his friend, "They must have followed us," he whispered.

"Bring him to me," said Kashka to someone, presumably a soldier standing next to him outside.

The men inside heard the tramp of feet and then the glittering head of a javelin poked through the doorway, then cautiously a helmeted head, looking directly into the face of Barook.

Shelomo could see the look of surprise on the soldier's face as he saw the young man standing in the shadows with the sword at his side.

The glittering head of the javelin swung around toward Barook, who simply stood there, staring into the other man's eyes. Too late the soldier realized there must be someone else. The pummel of Marook's sword came down hard on the nape of the soldier's neck. The soldier's armor clanged as it hit the stone floor.

Shelomo and Marook made quick eye contact. Shelomo nodded. Both men realized that they only had moments in which to fight back before they lost the advantage of surprise. Marook charged from the door of the change room toward the three figures standing in the fading light just inside the shrine's entrance way. The blacksmith struck the first of them with the sharp edge of his sword, a downward stroke from his powerful shoulders that caught one of the soldiers between neck and chest. The soldier fell without a sound. Kashka gave a high-pitched yelp and sidled backwards, clutching for the dagger at his side. The remaining soldier with Kashka recovered quickly, leveled his javelin, and jabbed expertly at Marook. The javelin pierced Marook's abdomen, and he went down clutching at the javelin. The soldier let it go and drew his sword in a fluid motion.

Barook cried out as he saw his father fall and swung his sword with all his might at the soldier—a wild arc of bronze. The soldier stepped backwards to avoid the blow and barreled into Kashka, who reeled backwards awkwardly. Barook, unbalanced now, stumbled and fell onto his knees; his sword struck the floor with a bright flash of sparks and skittered away, over the smooth pebble surface of the square. Shelomo rushed forward, sword at the ready. With a deft step Shelomo inserted himself between his fallen comrades and their foe— *this was a mess. Any moment a patron would walk through from the baths to investigate the ruckus, or a eunuch would raise the alarm,* he thought.

With an arcing strike he tried to split the helmeted skull of the soldier. The soldier recovered quickly and parried Shelomo's first blow expertly. Breathing harshly now, he faced Shelomo, a look of fierce concentration on his face. Shelomo knew he faced a master swordsman. Their initial advantage of surprise was over.

The soldier circled, holding Shelomo's gaze, "Old man, you are already dead," he said fiercely, sword at the ready. Now Shelomo knew he was fighting for his own life. Out of the corner of his eye he saw Kashka pick up the fallen soldier's sword.

"Barook! Watch out!" he cried as Kashka rose with sword in hand and stepped toward Barook. Barook slid back helplessly on his buttocks; his sword lay several yards to his left. For a moment all three men froze and then everything happened with a flurry that was hard to follow. Barook lunged for his fallen sword and at the same moment, almost unnoticed, a small shadow sped from the darkness of the shrine's doorway.

Kashka, with a piercing scream of triumph, rushed in to deliver a death blow to Barook, and at the same moment the soldier Shelomo fought lunged at him.

Shelomo fell back, desperate to try to save Barook. He saw Kashka, sword raised above his head, but the triumphal scream had changed to a gag and now issued from the lips of a dying man. From the center of Kashka's chest protruded the shaft of a javelin. Kashka looked down at it stupidly and then into the fierce green eyes of a little boy, breathing hard holding the other end. The soldier confronting Shelomo looked on with astonishment. The tip of his sword wavered. Shelomo saw the opening. The flat of his sword rang against the soldier's helmeted head. The soldier crashed to the floor unconscious. At almost the same instant, in an obscene caricature of choreography, Kashka took two tottering steps and hit the pebbled surface, forehead first and stone dead.

Breathing hard, Shelomo let his sword sink to his side.

"Are you all right, Yeshua?" he said.

The boy nodded, and then turned to his father, tears beginning to stream from his eyes. Barook already sat at his father's side holding the man's big shaggy head in his lap. The night breeze sighed through the shrine opening, stroking Marook's beard.

Barook looked up at his little brother, a look of fierce pride in his eyes.

"You saved my life little brother," he said thickly.

"And mine," came a hoarse whisper.

"Father!" both boys said at once. A look of sheer delight crossed their faces.

Marook smiled and then grimaced.

Shelomo raced over. Squatting at Marook's side he gently inspected the wound.

"The rope around your stomach has saved you," he said. "Look! The tip of the javelin has sliced into your side, but not too deeply. No, don't remove the rope Barook, that is keeping the wound shut."

"Help me up," Marook said.

With the aid of his sons and his friend he stood up on shaky legs, then using the javelin to lean on he said, "This is a mess. The guard will be here any moment with all that screaming going on."

Shelomo gave a short laugh. "Perhaps, but does it not strike you as odd that the eunuch on duty is not where he should be and neither are any of the sconces lit. I have never had much faith in the Babylonian eunuch, but this is passing strange. It has worked in our favor. Still, we should not hang around. Barook, use that unconscious soldier's sashes to tie up their hands and then help me to dump the body of the dead soldier and the eunuch into the latrine. Yeshua you draw a bucket of water from the cistern and wash down some of that blood and hurry! Then come back and help your father back to the house."

"But what about the orb?" Marook said.

"Things have played into our hands," said Shelomo. "Think about it. These dead bodies will rot quickly in the pit. With that awful stench they will think the god has turned on them and they will fill that latrine up as quickly as possible to rid the temple of the smell and the sacrilege, thus burying the orb. The only people who know where the orb is are us and Obrahim and he will not be back any time soon, one would think."

"But what about the soldiers? Shall we kill them?" Barook said.

"No!" Shelomo said sharply. "Those who died tonight, we killed in self defense. That is permissible. If we killed the unconscious soldiers that would be murder. The Lord of Hosts does not allow such things."

Barook's face fell.

Shelomo patted his shoulder.

"It will not be necessary, Barook. Consider what would happen to the soldiers should they go back to the high priest and report their failure? You know that they would be instantly killed. No, these men are far shrewder than that. They will simply say that the eunuch dismissed them and they went home

The Flame of Heaven

while their friend, the soldier who died, stayed with Kashka, and they will deny any knowledge of his whereabouts. Or if they are honest men, which I doubt, they will slink away into the desert and sell their services to some other Lord."

Marook chuckled weakly.

"So . . . the orb is safe for a time. And what of us, Shelomo?"

"I think it would be prudent for you and your family to take a long trip to Nineveh to do some profitable trade and visit your family. As for me, this will be my last night in Babylon. My Lord wants me elsewhere."

Marook looked at his friend searchingly in the dim light cast by the flickering glow of the lamps in the houses surrounding the temple complex. A faint shiver ran down his spine as he looked into those ancient eyes.

"Dare I ask where you are going?" Marook said gruffly.

Shelomo smiled. "You may. All that has been revealed to me is what I have already told you. I am to go north, to make my home among the barbarians for a time."

Marook sank slowly to his knees and made his boys do likewise.

"Marook what is it? Are you feeling faint? Do not give up, we will get you back home."

From his position on his knees Marook looked up at the strange man he knew only as Shelomo.

"My friend, I am fine. I will survive. This night has taught me something far stranger than I ever imagined. It has taught me that there truly is a great God, a God above all gods as you have said to me many times—and that he is a God who can be trusted, who looks with compassion upon men. This night I pledge to your God my life and the life of my sons. We are now your servants."

Shelomo smiled, tears brimming in his eyes.

"My God has heard and accepts you, because of your great faith. You shall serve his purposes in this land. Now come men, let us make haste."

Chapter 26

Faisal parked the Peugeot, extracted a black carryall bag from the back and walked slowly along the darkened suburban road. He avoided the pools of weak halogen light from the streetlights. Somewhere to his left a dog barked halfheartedly at the rising moon.

He stopped in front of the Zimmerman's home. The house was dark, except for the porch light. He could hear the tinny voice of the TV presenter reading the seven o'clock news, catching something about a Syrian buildup of arms near the Golan Heights and several Hezbollah missile strikes in the north of the country in response to the bomb attack, which had killed the leader of Hezbollah.

Things are hotting up already and they are about to get much, much hotter, he thought.

He strode into the garden, listening, considering how to kill Rebeccah Zimmerman. *Knife or gun?* He preferred a clean kill. *I'm a rifleman and besides a lot of these Jewish bitches have military training, some of them know how to handle themselves.*

He stopped, squatted on his haunches, out of sight behind the waist-high fence, unzipped the carry bag and took from it a Glock pistol. He fished around inside the carryall and came out with a small silencer . . . *that should do.*

Rebeccah stood at the sink, pushing down the used dishes into the foaming water. They made a slight clinking sound as

The Flame of Heaven

she dabbed at them with the sponge. She pushed a stray lock of chestnut-colored hair back over her right ear.

In the dark Faisal swallowed hard. She looked so much like one of his own cousins. He rubbed his eyes, his jaw bunching involuntarily several times.

Rebeccah thought of her husband and smiled slightly to herself. A scratching at the door and the dog's whining broke her reverie. She sauntered over and opened the screen door on its rusty hinges.

"Moshie, what's wrong, boy? Where is your Master?" Rebeccah bent down and patted the dog.

"Moshie, what's wrong?" The little black dog, of indeterminate parentage, slunk into the house, shivering, with his bushy tail between his legs.

Faisal strode into the light spilling from the back door and onto the small lawn that ran to the high concrete fence at the rear of the house.

"Move inside," he said in broken Hebrew.

Rebeccah's breath caught in the back of her throat as her gaze took in the young Arab in his balaclava mask and the silenced gun.

The dog whined.

"My husband is just outside, if I were you I would leave quickly," she said evenly.

In Faisal's mind the picture of pathetic trust was too much. He grinned and then snorted a laugh.

"No, no, not so. You husband is dead. I killed him. You will join him soon."

Rebeccah's eyes blazed with unmitigated hatred as she looked up at the masked man from her squatting position.

Faisal laughed again and raised the pistol, looking deep into Rebeccah's eyes.

A tear ran from the corner of Rebeccah's right eye. She bit her lower lip. Lifting her face, she closed her eyes and said calmly.

"Then go ahead . . . you will get what you deserve."

She waited a few moments, with her eyes closed, expecting the sledgehammer blow of a bullet into her skull. Instead she heard a grunt and a thud.

She opened her eyes. Faisal lay in front of her, his gun hand outstretched, the pistol still in his grip. Behind him stood what Rebeccah later described to the police as an "apparition"— the outline of a man, in silver, but no features to speak of, or features that seemed to move in a grotesque flow across the oval of its face.

"Rebeccah," said a deep, warm male voice inside her skull.

Rebeccah felt terror surge through her mind. She barely managed to stifle a scream.

"Rebeccah . . . do not be afraid," said the voice again. "The things that will soon come to pass must be so."

Tears streamed down Rebeccah's face.

"My husband?"

"His body is dead, but he himself is safe . . . you are of the Way."

A warm glow suffused Rebeccah's breast and seeped into her shivering limbs.

"This man will not harm you now. Call the police."

As if with a flick of a switch, the angel vanished.

Rebeccah found her feet, sobbing in involuntary gasps. Her legs felt unsteady. She walked slowly to the phone and dialed the emergency number.

Chapter 27

The temple mount was well lit by the spotlights at the base of the Wailing Wall and the bank of bright halogens that ran the whole length of the mount. The Dome of the Rock mosque, like an alien form, sat squat on the base of what would have been the Jewish temple floor.

Getting onto the temple mount with the equipment had been challenging. The two bribed Waqf guards had finished placing the last of the equipment in prearranged spots just moments ago. Smuggling the bags through the ancient underground tunnels in the mountain and storing them in nooks had been difficult to do without detection and had taken the better part of a week.

Dupree and his men went up the ramp in twos and threes and were simply waved through by the Israeli police guard. Dupree and two others came up last behind a bunch of loud American tourists. Bribing the two Waqf had been difficult enough; they had not bothered with the idea of bribing Israeli police. The Israeli police ran armed patrols on the mount at night while the Waqf left after dark. There was no love lost between the Waqf guards and the Israeli police. The authorities had worked out long ago that having armed Israelis and Palestinians in the same confined area was not a good idea. This knowledge had played directly into Dupree's plans.

Dupree walked slowly toward one of the many broken walls of ancient buildings which dotted the mount. In the gloaming light he found the backpacks where they should be.

Slowly, the other men arrived at the rendezvous. Compact automatic weapons were quickly retrieved from the bags and secreted in jacket pockets. Dupree fitted his earpiece and blew experimentally into the microphone as he walked away from the group. The men melted away in all directions, obediently going to their prearranged points.

"Report in," he said softly into the microphone.

The signal to clear the mount for the night chimed and groups of tourists moved off toward the rear of the mount and the steps that would take them to its base.

A temple mount policeman walking slowly toward Dupree said, "Sir, it is time to leave for the night. We open again . . ."

Dupree shot the man in the chest through his coat pocket.

The policeman sat down hard on his buttocks, looking up with a shocked expression from the seeping stain in the middle of his chest into the hard face of the man that had just murdered him.

Dupree cleared his throat, looked around to see if anyone had noticed; no one had, or not just yet. He made brief eye contact with the man covering him, then nonchalantly walked over to a fuse box responsible for the lighting on the mount and put a rapid succession of bullets through it. This action certainly got people's attention as the fuse box exploded and the halogens blinked off, then on, then off again. A group of tourists rounded the corner of the mosque followed by another Israeli policeman. The policeman's eyes swept over the scene before him as he leveled his automatic weapon at Dupree.

"Hey, you! Stay where you are!" he shouted out in Arabic.

Dupree watched as the left side of the policeman's handsome young face erupted in a mush of gore and blood. The gunman behind him swung his silenced pistol on the group of tourists and yelled, "Run, run for your lives! We are bringing about the end of days!"

The women in the group of tourists screamed and the men tried to put themselves between their womenfolk and the gunman. All over the temple mount, groups of tourists ducked for cover, or ran as fast as they could for the Mughrabi Gate.

One of the tourists, an older man, said to the gunman, "Please sir, we mean no harm, we are tourists."

"Run, in the name of Christ, run, or you will die!" screamed the young thug in heavily accented English.

In a grotesque caricature of people trying to run as fast as they could, while avoiding being shot in the back, the group of middle-aged, overweight tourists galumphed toward the exit, two of the women screaming as they passed the body of the dead policeman. From the other side of the Dome, Dupree heard automatic gunfire. Pandemonium broke out all over the mount, as all the tourists rushed toward the gate.

Dupree ignored the rushing bodies, and put another few bullets into the fuse box. Now just a faint glow reached the top of the mount from the spotlights below.

Automatic gunfire again. Dupree squatted, and from his other pocket he retrieved the headpiece of his night-vision goggles and pulled it on over his head. Twenty meters away he could see his henchman doing the same thing.

"Anwar, one of our men is in trouble," barked Dupree into his lapel microphone. "Silence that automatic fire."

The man from across the way nodded and sped around the hexagon of the Dome of the Rock mosque.

Another burst of automatic weapons fire and the plop, plop of silenced gunfire, then all was silent.

"Report in! We must have a body count of five temple policemen!"

A faint crackle issued from Dupree's headpiece as the various men around the temple mount reported in.

"Any of ours dead or wounded?"

None dead, one slightly wounded. Better than expected, thought Dupree.

To the wounded man Dupree said in fluent Arabic, "Number three, drop your weapon and leave with the tourists. Meet us back at the safe house. The Waqf at the gate will not stop you."

"Four and five, is the body attached?"

"Yes!" came the brusque reply.

"Okay, winch away. Once it is up, place it near the building. The rest of you place our explosives and kill anyone who tries to stop you, then meet back at the winch on the western side of the building."

Dupree checked his watch . . . one minute had gone since the first bullet fired. He knew he would not have more than another couple of minutes and then he was as good as dead.

He and Anwar headed in a crouching run for the western side of the building. Faint screams and sounds of confusion could still be heard from the exit; otherwise an eerie calm had settled over the jumble of buildings on the temple mount. Dupree turned to Anwar, a grin on his face, "I liked the—in the name of Christ bit you pulled there—the end of days." He pulled a face, then laughed out loud.

"A nice piece of propaganda that is sure to be widely publicized."

The men rallied around the small winch that had been attached by one of the bribed Waqf temple mount guards. It was secured via a looped rope around one of the ancient pillars jutting from the mount; the dead body of Zimmerman lay in fatigues ten yards away, a Tavor rifle next to his right hand.

"Good work men." Dupree removed his goggles and looked into the dark faces of the men round him.

"Don't look so worried. Allah will understand. You know that all is made righteous to defeat the infidel. The Dome will be rebuilt; the funds have already been secured for this purpose. Nazrallah must be avenged. The only way we can defeat Israel is to draw her into war with the whole of Islam. Destroying the Dome will do it. You can be sure of that. No one will believe that Israel is innocent after Nazrallah's death. The world will simply think that extremist elements among the Israelis are out to make trouble and take advantage of the heightened tensions."

The young men nodded as one.

Dupree smiled, pulled one of the nearest young men to him and attached a short bit of rope that extended from his vest to a belay hook. The rest followed suit. "The winch will get you down in no time. Secure the area below, but do not make yourselves conspicuous. Once Anwar and I are down, split up and meet back at the house."

"Allah Akba!"

"Allah Akba!" they all shouted, as the first of them disappeared over the dark face of the west side of the mount, the winch whining under the strain.

Dupree looked at his watch again . . . two minutes since the first shot.

"Listen Dupree!" said Anwar, a note of fear in his voice.

On the evening breeze the faint thud, thud of a chopper's blades could be heard.

"We don't have much time . . . you're not going to crack up on me now, Anwar?" said Dupree through a sneer.

Anwar scowled at the Algerian.

The last of the other men disappeared over the side of the western wall.

"Go and undo the winch coupling and throw it over the edge."

Dupree pulled a mobile phone from his pocket, pressed his code into the number pad and placed the phone in an upright position on the ground.

Anwar made sure the last of the men made it to ground level, then threw the winch and coupling off the edge. Dupree stepped up behind him, tightened the straps of his carryall on his back and checked the buckle around his waist. He took the tip of a black cord that ran from the carryall on Anwar's back and said, "Make sure you take a long jump, there are stones that jut out from the side."

Anwar took five quick steps and jumped over the edge silently. A black ball of material snapped out over his head, pushed out by the percussive at the bottom of his pack. They had practiced these low base jumps many times, but Dupree had some reservation about Anwar's nerve. He had seen some pretty horrific parachute mishaps and they really did not have time for mishaps.

The scented night breeze caught in the material, and Anwar floated out above the Kidron Valley below. Dupree looked over the edge briefly. The chute was full and Anwar floated gently on the night breeze. The Glock in his hand twitched. He felt an almost overwhelming compulsion to kill Anwar as he floated down. He struggled for a moment and managed to resist.

Dupree looked at the face of the mobile phone at his feet . . . thirty seconds. The thud of the helicopter grew more distinct.

Those Israeli Special Forces were going to meet with one hell of a surprise, he thought and smiled.

He took three quick steps and threw himself off the temple mount into the embrace of the black night sky above Jerusalem.

Chapter 28

Rebeccah's hands were cuffed as she was led from the cell into which she had been shoved in the early morning. They had taken her shoes away from her.

Her mind felt fuzzy from lack of sleep and grief as she tried to make sense of the night before. The police had been kind to her at first. They took the gunman away and asked her to give a statement, which she did and of course they did not believe her. They asked her to come down to the station with them. Then they asked her a lot of questions about where her husband was. She told them what the gunman had said. They allowed her to rest for a little while at the station. Later, they had woken her from a troubled sleep and taken her to another place in the back of a police van.

Behind Rebeccah, following at a regulated distance, was a man with a Tavor assault rifle; in front was a woman she guessed would be her interrogator, slightly older than she—bottle blonde, dark roots showing and tired looking. Rebeccah's feet made slight squeaking sounds as she walked across the gloss surface of the linoleum floor.

She was led into a room with small windows, high in the wall looking out onto a bright Jerusalem spring morning. The room contained a metal table bolted to the floor; a fold-up camp chair and a stool faced each other across the table. High on the wall facing the stool was a TV screen.

She had had nothing to eat or drink since the ordeal the night before and felt faint and like she needed to go to the toilet.

"Could I go to the . . ."

"Quiet!" barked the older women in Hebrew. "Traitors get nothing."

"What are you talking about?" said Rebeccah frowning.

I must look a mess, she thought. She had been crying all night and she felt her eyes to be puffy and her face felt hot.

"Sit!"

Rebeccah sat obediently on the metal stool behind the gunmetal gray table. The linoleum floor reflected the bright sunlight lancing in through the small windows. A double-tube fluorescent light buzzed brightly overhead. In one corner of the room, there was the bright silver eye of a drain. The man with the Tavor stood at the door in his fatigues, staring at her impassively. A thrill of fear stabbed Rebeccah's heart. She knew what this place was. These were the holding cells of Shin Bet, the counterterrorism defense ministry of Israel. In the hush of the room she heard the first of the far away gunshots and screams.

"What's going on?" said Rebecca in English.

"Like you don't know," said the woman in Hebrew. The woman pointed a remote control at the TV set and it burst to life. Smoke rose over Jerusalem. A helicopter shot of the temple mount showed the smoldering wreck of the Dome of the Rock, the news channel was CNN, in English. An excited voice said: " . . . this is the work of an extremist Christian group calling itself the Meggido Army or Armageddon Army. A statement sent to a CNN website claimed that their aim was to speed the Lord's return by ushering in the New Jerusalem. This will be achieved, they say, when a new temple is built on the holy site. They add that it is regrettable that confrontation between Israel and her enemies is inevitable. A statement released by the head of the Arab League said that if Israel does not immediately distance itself from this group and allow the Dome to be rebuilt, she will be attacked. The president of Iran has called on all Muslim nations to unite under Iranian leadership and attack Israel. In a statement released by the Knesset, the prime minister of Israel has called for calm and has stated that the Israeli security forces have had nothing to do with this incident. He however, did release this stark warning to the enemies of Israel."

What followed terrified Rebeccah. The prime minister spoke candidly of Israel using all disposable means to protect her citizens and her territory should that be necessary, including weapons of mass destruction.

The commentator broke in and said that while it was not officially confirmed that Israel possessed atomic weapons, the reference to weapons of mass destruction could be interpreted as a veiled reference to nuclear warheads.

Rebeccah looked with confusion at her interrogator and was about to speak.

"Quiet Rebeccah . . . there is more."

Once again Rebeccah turned to the TV.

She saw the bald head of an Englishman speaking pacifying words, the chief prosecutor of the International Court with pasty face and dead eyes, then dear God, a photograph of her husband in military uniform and the accusation that he had something to do with the destruction of the Dome.

"Never fear, we will get to the bottom of this. We will bring the perpetrators of this horrendous crime to book and the international community will know justice," said the Englishman.

"I have it on good authority that already Shin Bet has several suspects in custody."

A picture of the Shin Bet headquarters from the air sprang onto the screen, the place she believed she now sat.

"In related news an extremist Jewish sect has tried to place the foundation stones of the new Jewish temple they hope to build on the mount. Two members of the sect were shot dead by Israeli security forces when they tried to storm the Mughrabi Gate with the foundation stones."

The TV snapped off.

"My name is Alte Cohen. I am your best friend or your worst enemy, Rebeccah," said the older woman in a steady, low voice.

Rebeccah looked into the steely blue-green eyes confronting her across the table and for a second time felt a thrill of fear run through her.

"I swear to Almighty God, I do not know what this is all about!" said Rebeccah with vehemence, as tears sprang unbidden from her eyes and coursed down her cheeks.

"Almighty God?" said Alte. "That is interesting. This is the Christian God, is it not?"

Rebeccah stared at the woman, her lips trembling.

"I don't understand?"

"Let me paint a picture for you. You and your husband are both Christians, you belong to one of those evangelical Christian cults who believe in the second coming of Christ and you are responsible for trying to foment war between Israel and her enemies."

"No, no! I love Israel. I am a Jew."

"No, you are not; you have turned your back on your community. You did so when you became a Christian and . . ."

Anger flared in Rebeccah's heart. This was the usual Jewish bigotry aimed at Christianity. "Nonsense, we are Messianic Jews. We merely believe in fulfilled Judaism. Christians are the inheritors of the Abrahamic promises. We worship and serve the God of our Fathers."

"Does that include fomenting war between Israel and her enemies? Your husband's body was found on the mount with Israeli police bullets in it."

Rebeccah took several deep breaths to try to control herself from bursting into tears.

"My husband was murdered by a terrorist last night while walking our dog . . . his body was probably left there to be found. I called the police remember, or have you conveniently forgotten that fact. A Palestinian gunman tried to kill me!"

Alte began to chuckle to herself and then burst into laughter.

"Do you know? I almost believe you. But come, Rebeccah, how ridiculous. Tell the truth. The man found in your kitchen is not a Palestinian; he is an Arab from the UAE."

Alte looked at Rebeccah with contempt and skepticism etched in her eyes.

"You Christians believe in the truth, don't you? Do you know the names of the other men involved in this plot? No? Prove to me that you are a good Jew, as you call yourself. Tell me who they are. They murdered five policemen last night. Israeli policemen."

Rebeccah sat silently, looking into the merciless eyes in front of her.

"I want to speak to a lawyer."

"A what?"

"My lawyer. The last time I checked, I had rights."

Alte burst into laughter again and the man with the Tavor chuckled.

"No, Rebeccah you have no rights. You are the guest of Shin Bet. You have been arrested and detained under antiterrorist legislation. You can be held incommunicado indefinitely."

Now real fear seized at Rebeccah's throat and she began to pray fervently in her mind. *"My Lord and my God, what is going on? Please save me!"*

"Do we really need to bring your rabbi or your church into this Rebeccah? You love that old man like a father, don't you?"

Rebeccah's mouth compressed into a line of anger, "I have told you already, I do not know anything."

"You mean you were not involved in the plot, but you know about the plot?"

Rebeccah laughed bitterly, "Ah, I see now. You will twist my words. Well, I will say no more."

Alte gave a wintry smile.

"The name of the man found in your house is Faisal Habib. He has links to several terror groups. How did he come to be unconscious on the floor of your house? Maybe you betrayed your husband for a new lover?"

Rebeccah looked into the other woman's eyes. She launched herself across the table at those mocking eyes and tried to kick Alte in the face. Alte had been expecting a reaction and managed to skip out of her chair and across the floor.

Rebeccah landed in a heap on the floor on the other side of the table.

The guard with the Tavor stood over her, the barrel of the assault rifle a foot away from her head. Rebeccah glared up at them.

"Shoot! Go on, shoot me! I have nothing to live for now," screamed Rebeccah.

Tears coursed down her face.

Alte looked down at Rebeccah with a deep look of concentration in her eyes.

She stood that way for some time, and then said abruptly, "You must appreciate how strange this sounds to me Rebeccah . . . angels, acts of God. A plot by Arabs to blow up one of their most holy sites? Come? Even you Christians can appreciate how . . . unlikely that all is. "

The interrogator reached into the side pocket of her fatigues and extracted a black silk hood, then stepped around the table and gently placed the hood over Rebeccah's head and drew the strings at the bottom of the bag tight.

"I hope you are not claustrophobic, Rebeccah, silk is soft to touch, but very difficult to breathe through. We will be back this time tomorrow. Please think about what you want to say. We are especially interested in the link between your husband and Faisal Habib. Faisal is our guest too and I'm sure we will get him to speak. Whoever speaks first gets the favored treatment, possibly even a pardon if the information is good. You know how it works."

Rebeccah did not protest. She heard her persecutors leave the room and the door shut with a click. She rolled over onto her knees then stood carefully, walking a few paces trying to shake the bag from her head and flexing with all her might against the handcuffs. She felt a panic rising in her chest. She took three deep breaths and then sank to her knees and bowed over, weeping and praying silently.

Chapter 29

Shelomo woke with a start. He wiped at his brow, slick with sweat. He turned carefully in bed trying to extract himself from the tangled sheets. In the second single bed next to him, Lewis slept peacefully, his profile outlined in the gentle moonlight filtering through the shutter of their hotel room at the Palatine Hotel in old Jerusalem.

The rioting in the streets had subsided for the night. Feelings of anxiety Shelomo had been struggling with since the beginning of this upheaval boiled up in his heart.

He got up out of bed. Goosebumps rose over his bare chest and arms as the cool night breeze coming though the shutters played over him. He adjusted his boxer shorts and sighed. *What woke me?*

"*You are in danger,*" said the soft voice behind his left ear.

Shelomo jumped, despite having heard this voice many times. He spun around in the darkened room. The angel stood at a slight angle to the room floor, just to the right of the closed door to their room. Strange waves of colored light flickered across the sheen of the silver body.

Shelomo felt his knees go slightly weak.

You will have to move soon, said the voice inside his mind. *Kate will help carry a great burden in the next few days.*

Shelomo recovered quickly. Lewis moaned in his sleep and Shelomo's eyes darted across to Lewis's sleeping form.

Despite himself, he smiled. A very strong feeling of affection for his angel welled inside him.

The strange wave of light traveled up the angelic being's torso again.

What is going to happen to Kate, said Shelomo in his thoughts, but directing them at the angel. After many years of practice, this came to him almost by second nature now. *Can I not bare the burden for her?*

No. She will be called on to help another woman who is in great pain. The angel flickered again.

Why are you, er, flickering?

Without seeing any change to the angel's facial features, which were minimalist anyway, he felt it smile at him.

You are under severe attack . . . I am keeping the evil one at bay. Come, we do not have much time. Wake the others and pack your belongings into the vehicle downstairs. Once you have done that, drive directly to the corner of Patriarchate Street and David Street. That is not too far from here.

Shelomo smiled as he was then given a set of directions. He loved his angel's practical nature. In the many years of his life on earth he had been helped thousands of times that he was aware of, and no doubt countless times of which he was unaware.

You will meet a young woman called Rebeccah there. She will tell you where to go.

Why did we have to come to Jerusalem anyway? Was it to meet this woman, Rebeccah?

No answer. The silver man flickered twice. *Yes,* thought Shelomo, *as usual things not fully explained at first, were falling into place.*

Listen . . . I'm confused. I don't . . .

As you know Shelomo, all of the people with you have their use. We do not have time. Go and do as your Lord says, came the short reply.

The angel flicked off like a light.

Shelomo stood in the dark for a few moments, a little annoyed. There was no point in arguing with angels.

He turned and walked the two steps to Lewis and gently shook his arm.

He woke, "What time is it? What . . ."

"No time Lewis, my lad. I've just had some instruction from the Lord."

Lewis's eyes widened, "You mean the angel?"

"Yes," said Shelomo through a smile. The young people were still obviously unnerved by the angelic involvement. He could not blame them. Even after so many years, he too still had his moments with them.

"Our mission is taking shape. We are of course in danger, but the real business in Jerusalem has been revealed, and has nothing to do with Ashworth. We have to pick up a mysterious young woman called Rebeccah . . . and she is to be Katie's charge. Come, I'll explain as we go."

Chapter 30

Dekker slouched on the hotel room couch, flicking through the TV channels with a remote. Diagonally to his right Obrahim sat in an overstuffed wingback chair, staring into space; the face of the old professor slack, his eyes vacant and dark. Next to the door, at a small vestibule table to his left, a young gunman named Raphael sat, leaning against the wall. He had joined them two nights ago.

Dekker looked at the young man with a sideways glance. They had not spoken much. Raphael looked bored and was flicking his way through a porn magazine, stopping every now and again to ogle some titillating scene. His pistol lay on the table. Dekker found himself becoming irritated with the young thug's nonchalant self-absorption.

Raphael was young, about twenty. He wore his hair long and curly, and he had grown himself a mysterious little tuft of hair just below his lower lip.

Raphael looked up and caught Dekker's scrutiny. Dekker held his eyes.

"You want to use this magazine after I finish?" said Raphael in an indeterminate continental-accented English.

"Thanks, no. I'm not a wanker," Dekker said evenly.

Raphael's face remained blank. He shrugged and carried on flicking, ignoring Dekker's stare.

"You are bored, no? Maybe you and me go and rent some girls, hmm?" said the young man, with an amused pout playing around his lips.

Dekker ignored the comment; his eyes flicked to the balcony area. Outside Lord Ashworth stood with Dupree and the sergeant, speaking in low voices. While the words could not be heard, the tone of the conversation could be. Ashworth seemed to be praising, or encouraging Dupree. Dupree, in his way, looked glum and tired.

ಞ‍ಞ   ಞ‍ಞ   ಞ‍ಞ

The last several weeks had been nightmarish for Dekker, not knowing where Kate was and knowing all too well that he was a captive. He had at least one armed thug watching him all the time and he had been locked into his airless room at night while they remained at Ashworth's country estate. Many people, some whom he recognized from the political and judicial scene in England and some whom he did not, came and went. He was not introduced to any of them and was kept well away from the meetings between these people and Ashworth.

Ashworth had set them all a cracking pace of work. When he was available, which was usually late in the evenings, Lord Ashworth would question Obrahim. His questions centered around an object they finally settled on calling "the orb". Finally, weeks later, Ashworth decided on an archaeological expedition to the Middle East. The sergeant was put in charge of this project and the preparation of an archaeological expedition to ancient Babylon. Dekker was asked his opinion on certain technical details of the dig from time to time, but it was not his specialty, so he was gradually left out of the preparations. Indeed toward the end of their stay in England, it seemed that his usefulness was coming to an end. He wondered nervously what they had in store for him. Obrahim was in the clutches of severe culture shock, and while Dekker remained surly and uncooperative, he judged that he had some usefulness and the odds of his own survival were increasing.

What had most interested Dekker was the questions that Obrahim, the high priest, had asked them. Translating modern technology terms into ancient Babylonian had been almost impossible, so he'd set himself the task of teaching Obrahim some English and showing him things like a child.

Dekker, once a fully blown skeptic, had his world view thoroughly shaken as he found out more about Obrahim. His mind was a turmoil of resistance, disgust and desperate belief. During his time at the château he'd been given free reign in the library and had found a surprising and refreshing relief in the Bible. Professor Whitely himself had always been a skeptic and had passed that skepticism on to his students. Now Dekker found many of his previous humanistic assumptions shaken to the very core. If what he was experiencing was true, then the Bible was indeed historically accurate and if that was the case, then it would seem that the monotheistic view of the world it touted was not quite as absurd as it was presented at university.

One night the sergeant caught him reading the Bible in bed and had confiscated the book. She often invited herself into his room unannounced, no doubt in order to foil any nascent plans of escape. Dekker found that her presence nauseated him. She was oily and suggestive and rude all at once.

He had realized early that the only hope he had of seeing Kate again was through cooperation. He threw himself into his tasks, but all the while waiting for an opportunity to run. To date there had been no real opportunity; between Raphael, the sergeant, and Dupree, and the constant unnerving presence of Obrahim, he was going nowhere.

When they first arrived in Jerusalem it was without Dupree, and a wild thought of sprinting to the nearest consulate entered his mind. But it was soon extinguished by the realization that they were being watched by Israeli agents none too subtlely, and the new and unknown quantity of Raphael kept him in check.

ॐ ॐ ॐ

Raphael got up, put his pistol in his shoulder holster, checked that the door was locked and signaled to the sergeant standing on the balcony that he wanted to take a break.

Dekker's heart leapt.

Could he attack Raphael while he was on the toilet in a compromised position, take the key card and gun and get out of the hotel before . . . no too far fetched, he thought.

Sudden agitated movement in the professor broke his train of thought—the professor squirmed like a child in his seat, his face contorting horribly.

Was the professor still alive in there? Could he fight back? He hoped so.

"Professor?" Dekker said quietly. "Is that you?"

Angry eyes glared back at him.

"Your friend is in a very dark place, do not try to wake him." Obrahim said in his guttural tongue.

"Have you harmed him?" Dekker asked, his eyes flicking to the trio on the balcony. They were deep in conversation. Every now and then the sergeant looked in his direction, he guessed to make sure he was behaving. They had not heard him and Obrahim speaking.

Whitely pulled himself into an upright sitting position, eyes staring like a maniac. Then he crouched into a fetal position suddenly, as if his stomach hurt; his breathing became irregular and labored. Dekker knew what this meant. Obrahim was about to prophesy. Dekker purposely did not change his position, but allowed his eyes to flick up again. The trio on the balcony was distracted—deep in conversation. Something was afoot.

"She is here. She is here in Jerusalem. Stop them! Stop! They make their way by night to . . . to Petra," Obrahim spluttered in a hoarse whisper.

"Who is here?" Dekker said as casually as possible, but his heart hammered in his chest. *Could it be?*

The craggy old face lifted and blazing eyes stared at him.

"You! Traitor!" Obrahim choked. Dekker caught movement on the balcony in his peripheral vision and a moment later the toilet flushed.

"Who is she?" Dekker said again. He knew from experience that the prophet had almost no resistance to truth telling when in the trance state.

"Your woman and her friends make their way to Babylon. They go through Jordan. The same road, the same!" Tears trickled down the old face.

The Flame of Heaven

A burst of laughter from the balcony and then the glass door slid open.

Whitely sat upright again.

Dekker did not look up at the trio as they trooped into the living room. He did not want to betray the excitement and elation he felt at this moment. *Had they heard Obrahim prophesy?*

He flicked through several channels and turned up the volume. Something about the stock market tumbling on Wall Street.

"The sergeant, Raphael, Obrahim and you are leaving soon for Iraq," Ashworth said. He hesitated for a moment.

"Good god, Dekker, is Obrahim all right. He looks like he's just seen a ghost."

Dekker flicked his eyes up at Ashworth nonchalantly from where he sat.

"Yes, he's been a little agitated, sort of ants in his pants, but other than that, quite well behaved." Dekker said.

"Ask him if he feels well," Ashworth said. Dekker did as he was told.

The priest blinked several times and then stood up and walked unsteadily to the drinks cabinet.

"Get him a drink, Dupree," Ashworth said. "We really don't want him falling off his perch right now. After all, he will be leading the expedition, so to speak. He is the only one who knows where it is."

He paused, then turned and addressed Dekker, "Did he say anything?"

Dekker hoped that the emotions he felt were not visible, "Well, he did mumble something to himself a couple of times, but nothing I could make sense out of."

"Why didn't you call us, Dekker?" the sergeant said.

Dekker ignored her.

"What did he say?"

"Nothing intelligible . . . What? Look, there is another person in there after all. He does come across a bit odd from time to time. Sort of mumbles to himself, or the prof. Who knows?"

Ashworth held his eyes for several beats.

"Dekker, you know I'm a man you shouldn't cross, don't you?"

"I'm not a fool, Lord Ashworth," Dekker said, holding his gaze.

"I'll be the judge of that, Dekker. If he says anything and I mean anything; I want to know. Do you understand?"

Dekker looked at the trio and Raphael as he entered, still holding his porn magazine. The hatred that he felt for these people threatened to overwhelm him. His eyes darted to the front door.

"Yes, I understand," Dekker said, then looked away and changed the channel.

Chapter 31

The door lock gave off a percussive click. Rebeccah looked up from where she kneeled, her head still inside the silk hood. There was a sudden feeling of release around her wrists. The titanium handcuffs fell with a loud chink onto the linoleum floor, then Rebecca heard the TV overhead fizz into life.

She scrambled to her feet and yanked the silk bag off her head.

A silver glow emanating from the TV screen cast an eerie luminescence around the darkened room.

"Rebeccah," said the TV softly.

Rebeccah's breath caught in her throat. A sense of unreality made her feel momentarily weak in the knees. She leaned heavily on the table.

"Yes!" she said in a soft whisper.

"I want you to walk quickly from here. Look neither to your left or right. Do not answer anyone if they should speak to you. Take a right into the corridor and walk to the end. There you will see a door in front of you; it is the fire escape. Take the stairs all the way down. Three flights, and wait at the door at the bottom of the stairs. When you hear the door open, walk through immediately. Once you are through that door turn left up the hill and go to the corner of Patriarchate Street and David Street in the old quarter. There you will meet a young English woman called Katie. Take her and her friends to Rabbi Gurion. You are to leave the city tonight and go via Jordan to Baghdad."

"Yes, my Lord," Rebeccah said.

The TV flicked off.

Rebeccah walked to the door; a momentary sense of unreality passed over her as she pushed down the door handle and the door swung open silently. The corridor was lit by a row of recessed buzzing fluorescent lights reflecting brightly off the plastic floor. The surface of the floor was so bright after the darkened room it looked like water reflecting sunlight. Rebeccah took a right and walked quickly and silently down the corridor. Except for the slight buzzing of the lights and the sigh of the air conditioning, there was not a sound. Doors painted gun-metal gray stood to attention, like sentries, every few feet. The corridor she walked down intersected another. She paused and stealthily looked right and then left, hesitating just momentarily. As she did so, a door opened at the left end of the intersecting corridor and a man dressed in military fatigues and shouldering a Tavor stepped through.

He turned momentarily to close the door.

Rebeccah jumped across the intersecting corridor, her feet making a slapping sound when she landed. She knew her hesitation had blown it. Rebeccah ran toward the door up ahead marked "Exit".

"Hey! Hey you! Stop!" She heard footfalls coming rapidly toward her. Rebeccah made the door and yanked it open. She expected an alarm to sound, but it did not. She looked back over her shoulder. A crouched figure came hurtling around the corner, the barrel of the assault rifle now pointing up; it arced in her direction as the door closed behind her. She heard the lock mechanism click into place. Fists pummeled the door and muted shouts echoed over her head as she flew down the stairs in great leaps. Her knees gave way on the second landing and she fell heavily, thudding with force into the wall. Her pulse was a roar of sound in her ears. Up again. Adrenaline flooded her body. She clutched for the handrail and scrambled down the last flight of stairs.

This was all going terribly wrong.

Great sobbing gasps wrenched themselves from her lungs.

At last! The door. Nowhere to go, but straight ahead. Overhead she heard the static of walkie-talkie feedback, voices and pounding boots in the stairwell. The door before her clicked loudly. She wrenched it open with all her strength.

Close the door after you, said a cool voice in her mind.

A dark figure came hurtling down the last bend in the stairway just as Rebeccah slammed the door shut.

Rebeccah's long hair flew around her head as she took her bearings— *David Street was not far away.* The door in front of her rattled violently in its frame as the guard behind it kicked at the lock mechanism. She could hear the frantic static of electronic communication through the door. She turned left and sprinted for all she was worth, up the lamp-lit street, the dark night air cold and still carrying the slightest acrid odor of tear gas.

Chapter 32

Rebeccah sat in the back of the Land Rover, her head resting on a bunched-up sweater stuffed between her shoulder and the SUV's vibrating window. She felt emotionally numbed, distant, as if another person experienced her pain and fatigue. The scenes from the night before streamed phantasmagorically through her mind, played over and over again. The woman who sat next to her and held her hand—Kate—had immediately taken her into her arms as she came running along David Street. She sighed as she remembered how she had clung to this stranger and sobbed, great wrenching sobs.

Kate bundled her into a warm jacket and into the car. There were others, a discussion, an older man, several younger men, another woman—she no longer cared. The old man's face bobbed into view. "Are you Rebeccah?" She nodded, and through wracking sobs she told the man everything: her husband had been murdered, they had tried to kill her, and the authorities thought she was a terrorist. The old man looked at her with compassion. She could tell he believed her.

"Did an angel tell you how to find us? Where to go? We're stuck here in Jerusalem, no flights in or out, the borders are closed."

From deep inside her numbed mind, she remembered what the voice said.

"My rabbi, Gurion." She gave the man the Rabbi's private number. "My rabbi will help you."

The Flame of Heaven

The old man made the phone call. A quick discussion, a rendezvous arranged. Then they were all somehow in the car, Kate had simply held her like she was a baby, shivering and wretched. She had felt the other woman's tears falling onto her hair. Just the steady drip of quiet tears had comforted her.

The SUV they were in was parked in a dark laneway for about half an hour. Another SUV with the older man had gone on. She and Kate talked a little. Kate poured her a cup of hot coffee from a thermos. She learned that Kate had lost her husband too, possibly dead.

The journey through the darkened Jerusalem streets resumed. Now going slowly, in circuitous routes, avoiding the roadblocks and main streets, once or twice, swiftly stopping, as helicopters hammered overhead with their searchlights flicking the streets and walls; they were following someone.

Once they had crossed into the West Bank things became quieter. The convoy came to a halt. More quick, quiet discussions. Up ahead she saw her rabbi's face in the SUV headlights. He spoke with the older man—Shelomo. The rabbi seemed to be giving them some sort of direction and a map, then he came with his old man's stoop to her open window. She smiled up at him through her tears.

"Child, you are safe with these people. I'm so sorry for your loss. The Lord's Angel came to me. You must lead these people now. You know the way, by the old road south of the Banaai Kibbutz? Go, I know you are innocent. Do not worry about me."

She nodded and sobbed. She caught a few words "Babylon", "archaeological digs"; the older man clearly in charge—who were these people? Kate had not left her; that was a comfort.

Still later that night they crossed rough country into Jordan. The borders were pretty porous and almost impossible to police effectively. She knew the kibbutz well. She had lived there with her parents as a child.

Andrew P. Wright

Now she looked out into the bleak gray of a desert dawn, the SUVs' traveling fast along Jordan's well-kept highways. Their destination, Baghdad. Iraq was still occupied by the Americans, despite their new president's best efforts to extricate American troops, and still dangerous, especially for foreigners.

Chapter 33

Lord Ashworth looked deeply into the eyes of the Minister for Security in Israel.

"Perhaps I'm not understanding you, Minister. Are you telling me that the only suspect you have in relation to the Dome—fiasco—is missing?"

"Yes, sir, that is what I'm telling you. But we have made several more arrests overnight, other members of her Church, including her rabbi. We are questioning them," said the minister through a stony expression.

"But how? What? How can I possibly finish my enquiry without being able to question the primary suspect," Ashworth blustered.

"Sir, we know this is an embarrassment to Israel, but we are trying to cooperate. We have arrested all those people closest to the suspect and we have questioned them ourselves, very closely. There does not appear to be any . . . ah, fundamentalist connection."

Ashworth looked down his nose at the man in front of him.

"We have Jewish fundamentalists storming the Mughrabi gate, trying to lay foundation stones, and fundamentalist Christians singing hymns at the Wall, proclaiming the end and you say there is no connection?"

"Nothing that can be reasonably connected to the attack," the Minister said, ignoring Ashworth's sarcasm.

"Except the dead body of an Israeli Christian paramilitary," Lord Ashworth said through a sneer.

The minister did not answer.

"You realize, I'm sure Minister, that any embarrassment Israel may suffer in relation to this, is infinitely preferable to, well, war."

The minister narrowed his eyes, "We have nothing to be embarrassed for, sir. Have you thought that there may be a faction among the Muslim extremists who may want to foment war with Israel . . ."

"Absurd!"

"Sir, with all due respect, you are being naïve. We uncover plots of one sort or another just about every week."

Lord Ashworth gave the minister his most withering stare.

"I'm going to try very hard to persuade the Syrians and the Iranians not to attack Israel. The best way for me to do that is to find a culprit—a guilty party."

The minister's eyes became hard. "We wish to find those responsible for this act and we will cooperate fully with any transparent and evenhanded investigation. I would add that we hope you succeed, sir, because Israel stands ready to defend herself, as we always have."

Lord Ashworth looked down and flicked open the thick dossier that lay on the table before him and gently turned a page.

"Tell me Minister, do you think there is a link between the assassination of Nasrallah and the destruction of the Dome? If so, what is the link? At both events we find our main suspects to be highly decorated Israeli military men. Do you think that is a coincidence, Minister . . . or just bad luck?"

The minister remained silent for two beats and steepled his hands, looking down at the thick document before him, the logo of the International Court stamped in bold royal blue on a glossy white background.

"We can only trust that the International Court would not jump to conclusions, or make political statements based on emotion, sir."

"The findings of my preliminary investigation into the assassination of Nasrallah will be announced in public tomorrow.

The Flame of Heaven

You have the brief before you, Minister; although the evidence is circumstantial, we do see a connection between the two events. Both of them seem to have been perpetrated by Christian extremists, connected to Israel in some way. In the assassination of Nasrallah, Christian Lebanese extremists blew themselves up and managed to kill Nasrallah and several hundred Hezbollah supporters at the same time, and . . ."

"It seems curious to me, Lord Ashworth, that the International Court would hear a charge of crimes against humanity brought by a known terrorist organization against Israel, while Israel suffers the same kind of attack on an almost daily basis," said the minister, his eyes bright with rage.

"As you so rightly point out, Minister, the acts are not dissimilar, only those who perpetrate them are different. One a terrorist organization and the other a legitimate State: the State of Israel. Clearly only one of these can be held accountable from a legal point of view. The charge that has been brought before the International Court is one of . . . aggression. If the court makes a finding against Israel, then it gets referred to the Security Council."

"Hezbollah has government representation in the Lebanese parliament. While they are not a governing body, they are, well, a political entity. It seems to me that you are splitting hairs, Lord Ashworth. I have told you already, we have cooperated in your investigation fully. Israel had nothing to do with either event . . . you will find no proof of Israeli involvement, because there is no proof," the minister said, his face a stony mask of controlled anger.

"Yes, but how can my finding be any different, Minister. Our only suspect to the Dome incident has mysteriously vanished, but we know has links to a Doomsday Christian group and the only other suspect, an Israeli Mossad agent, with known links to Lebanese Christian extremists . . . come, there is clearly enough here to proceed to trial . . . if there is nothing else?

The minister did not answer him, but simply sat stock still with steepled hands and held the gaze of Lord Ashworth.

"There is another suspect, Lord Ashworth. We have in our custody a young man from the UAE named Faisal Habib. He was found unconscious on the floor of Rebeccah Zimmerman's kitchen the night we arrested her . . ."

The minister had the satisfaction of seeing Lord Ashworth's face turn white.

"Why was I not informed of this? This seems altogether too convenient," Lord Ashworth said curtly.

"And yet true. Faisal Habib has known links to terror groups throughout the Middle East," said the minister through a smile.

"I should like to question the man," snapped Ashworth.

"We have not yet finished with our interrogation. When we have done so, you may have access to him."

"And when will you finish? You may not have noticed, but we are trying to avoid a war here," Ashworth said, his own voice now thick with suppressed rage.

"We will let you know. In the meantime Lord Ashworth, in the interests of justice, I should think that your dossier needs to be revised with this new information at the very least."

Lord Ashworth tossed the dossier he held into his briefcase and shut the lid with a snap, then stood.

"I have business in Iraq to attend to. I should be there for about a week. If I do not have access to this mysterious person by the time I'm finished in Iraq, then I will simply be forced to make my recommendations as they stand. I bid you good day, Minister."

Chapter 34

The hajibs were surprisingly comfortable to wear, but hot. The men were gathered around the kitchen table and all laughed uproariously as Kate, Kirsten and Rebeccah did a twirl around the kitchen. The lady of the house, Mrs. Marook, clapped her hands; she'd helped the western women into their hajibs and showed them how to adjust the head scarf. The women, Arab and Jewish Christians, wore head scarves to church and Rebeccah knew how to do the deft folds of a good head scarf, but had allowed Mrs. Marook to fuss. Mr. Marook looked on with great satisfaction. The Marook family were Christian Iraqis and old friends of the Cele Dei.

Shelomo had kept contact with the Marook clan through time—*this generation were particularly devout, which was a great blessing in these troubled times,* he thought.

"Yes, it works. You could easily pass for three Iraqi women and no one would be the wiser," said Mr. Marook.

"I'm not sure I'll ever get used to this, but it'll be a relief to be able to leave the house and do a bit of shopping," Kate said.

Declan chuckled again, "For Heaven sake, just remember to let Mrs. Marook, or Rebeccah do all the talking, or you'll give the game away."

Shelomo smiled. "Now it's your turn Declan, Lewis. Any decent Arab woman has a chaperone, so that is your role today."

Lewis and Declan smiled, then got up to go and change.

"Aren't you going to join us, Shelomo?"

"No, Mr. Marook and I will be heading out to the ruins of Babylon today. Those tunics are too fine for laborers."

The young men nodded and went into the next room and put on one each of Marook's son's spare tunics. Mr. Marook helped them don their headpieces.

"You are a bit white for Arabs, but you will pass. It is fortunate that you have an olive skin and dark eyes," he said.

The girls chuckled at Declan and Lewis good-naturedly as they walked into the kitchen again.

"Okay, this is good and has worked out well, praise God. You are too big a group to walk into the market together. I think Mrs. Marook and Kirsten and Lewis go together, and then Declan, Kate and Rebecca follow about four or five meters behind. Do not acknowledge one another. Mrs. Marook will do the talking in the first group. Rebeccah, you do the talking if you have to in the second. I understand your Arabic is quite good." Shelomo added this last in a fluent Arabic flourish.

"Yes, it is fine," said Rebeccah in Arabic.

Mrs. Marook clapped her hands again and gave Rebeccah a hug. Despite both women being Christian, there had been a little tension between them, but now that had disappeared. Rebeccah smiled.

"The market is two blocks away, you can go on foot. We don't want neighbors commenting on strange western vehicles. Mr. Marook's sons took the SUVs away to a garage early this morning and they'll stay there until we need them. I'm going with Mr. Marook to the Babylonian digs to see if I can get closer to the action. With any luck we will land some work as laborers; but it is a huge site with several digs going on and construction at the same time, so we may need to stay there for a while. Does everyone understand? We are all here for a reason, some of those reasons obvious, some obscure. We trust that the Lord will reveal our way forward." Shelomo paused and then added, "It is very possible, even probable that we may see some of the enemy. You know what is required of you . . .

no vengeance. Walk away, slowly. Do not engage them until I have an understanding of the situation." Shelomo turned to Lewis and Declan, "You may only engage them if they pose a threat . . . otherwise just leave as quickly as possible without causing suspicion."

There were solemn nods all around.

Chapter 35

The battered Datsun made its way through the downtown Baghdad traffic and then turned south onto the only highway leading into the desert and the great building site that was ancient Babylon. Babylon was being rebuilt into a theme park. A project started by Saddam Hussein, the former dictator of Iraq, it now continued under the auspices of the United Nations as a project to bring work to the beleaguered people of Iraq and its millions of unemployed.

Busloads of casual workers, men and boys of all ages, took whatever transport they could to get to the site, after celebrating the Sabbath at home. The site was two hours distant from the outskirts of the city; many men had been known to walk for days to get to it. There were many such groups trying to hitch rides.

Shelomo and Marook spoke in Arabic as they bowled down the dusty freeway, bursts of news interspersed by long silences. In truth, Marook mused to himself, despite having met Shelomo several times through the years, and the first of those times as a young boy, and despite Shelomo being a very gentle and inoffensive person, he felt spooked around this man. He loved Shelomo like a father, yet there was just something about him that was unnerving. It wasn't that the man had a great presence either, as one might expect, it was quite the opposite. It was the stillness, the quietness, almost the absence of presence that unsettled one. He had met Saddam Hussein once; one could not miss his presence. He too was a still man, but his

The Flame of Heaven

stillness was the stillness of a snake before it struck. This man, on the other hand . . .

"Your sons? Are they well? Do they make progress in the faith?"

"Yes, Father, they do," Marook said.

Shelomo smiled to himself. He found the polite epithet touching. It reminded him . . . *I've been among westerners for too long,* he thought.

"Yeshua, if I told you how much you remind me of the first Marook, a beautifully faithful man . . . I told him about God and his plans, or as much as I knew then, and without my bidding, and without hesitation, he pledged his family to God, for all generations. Without hesitation."

Shelomo smiled at the pinprick of tears in the other man's eyes, in such sharp contrast to his tough, leathery face, thickset shoulders and barrel chest. *Yes, they even looked the same.*

"Come, let us stop and pick some of these boys up. It would be selfish not to and it would look very strange to arrive at the site with only two men in a car."

"Yes, you are right, Father."

"You cannot call me that in front of the other men, Yeshua. Call me Shelomo," he said and grinned.

The other man grinned, nodded, and slowed the car.

As they slowed, a gaggle of young men came running up to the car holding money out before them and gesticulating wildly.

Shelomo wound down the window, "Are you men off to the building site?"

"Yes, we are!" came the chorus of replies and offers to pay for the ride.

"No need to pay, jump in, we are on our way there and hope to secure some work too."

There was a mad scramble for the back seat and when Shelomo turned in his seat, he saw five eager young faces grinning back at him, gap toothed. The young men were small and thin; years of malnutrition communicated itself from their weathered faces, but all beamed with joy, shouting their thanks.

One of the men, the last into the car, said, "My uncle is a foreman there, he pours cement. I will ask him if he needs some more help. Praise be to Allah for your kindness. May he bless you." Shelomo smiled, "That is good news. Praise Almighty God. As you can see, we are old men, past our prime, but we are willing. We have never tried to find work here before." Good-natured laughter filled the cabin of the car.

"What is your name?"

"Ali, sir."

"We are educated men, we can speak English. Perhaps your uncle needs translators for the men and the Whites. I mean translators that can throw cement too!"

"Yes!" came a chorus of response, "especially ones who can throw cement!"

Another gale of laughter.

The journey continued on in high spirits for some time. They discussed the merits of the ongoing American occupation.

"Whatever is said, it is true that we would not have work otherwise," Ali said definitively.

Shelomo nodded his agreement.

"See the dust cloud up ahead, sir?" he added suddenly. The car had banked a rise in the road and now they looked down into the vast flood plain of the Euphrates.

"Yes," said Shelomo.

"That is the new Babylon."

An ancient, but familiar feeling shocked Shelomo's heart as he looked up at the cloud of dust, like a great fist, balanced precariously in the early morning desert air. A pounding, roiling wave of utter despair and wistful longing threatened to overwhelm him. Memories flooded his mind. Once, about 150 years ago, when the ruins of Babylon had first been rediscovered, he had come out here, just to be sure the Flame of Heaven had not been disturbed. The attempt to uncover Babylon had progressed under human power then, not earth moving equipment as now, and there had been no real threat, or so he had thought, of the object's recovery. The incense burner was so small, in such an immense graveyard to the past and buried so deep. At that time cuneiform was barely understood and although many thousands of tablets had been unearthed, he'd comforted himself with the thought that the chance of finding any reference to the Flame of Heaven was small. Even now, he was led to believe, in many museums in Europe lay stacks of cuneiform tablets that had yet to be deciphered. Nevertheless he had kept watch after that dig, first in Berlin, later in London. After all, the rediscovery of Babylon had been made by a German. Not long after that dig his suspicions had been tweaked. There had been something exceedingly worrying about the colossal confidence and self-importance of the Nazis and their quick rise to power, as well as the well-publicized fact that Hitler himself was an occultist and anti-Semite. This converging of events had caused him to suspect they had found something. He was never able to verify this suspicion exactly. There had been rumors about what the Nazis had done in private. Perhaps they had found a reference to something, or some other occultist object of power. Hitler reminded him of another young man that had worried him. Alexander had tried to rebuild the ziggurat and at that time there was a strong chance they could have found the orb. Secretly he had been thankful when Alexander had passed on; there was something frightening about that young man's abilities and intensity.

    Things went quiet again after the Second World War. Later the Cele Dei in Jerusalem had picked up some excitement among scholars in that city—ancient non-canonical Hebraic texts about Elijah, curiously never made known to the public, were unearthed in Sidonia. The Cele Dei were never able to penetrate that mystery and so started to keep careful note of those students who excelled in Sumerian and Akkadian languages around the world. It was quite easy to do, there were so few. Both Whitley and Dekker were monitored from time to time. Then the excavations in Babylon had resumed in earnest, generating new excitement among Akkadian scholars. Shortly afterwards Whitely had curiously disappeared from view for months, finally surfacing in Jerusalem and then again in

London. The Cele Dei had managed to find Kirsten a place in the British Museum, close to Sibyl Hardacre, and bam! What a discovery, almost by accident, although after all these years, Shelomo mused, I don't believe in accidents.

"Babylon the Great," Shelomo said suddenly, choking on the last word.

Yeshua glanced across at Shelomo as he nosed the Datsun into the chaos of vehicles on the outskirts of the site. Men poured from buses, trucks and battered cars. Silence fell over the men in the Datsun as they drew up next to the first of the mounds of dust and rubble.

Chapter 36

Kate, Declan and Rebecca paced about five meters behind the group comprised of Kirsten, Lewis and Mrs. Marook; the older lady reveled in her status as tour guide and was talking quietly but almost constantly to Kirsten, who nodded her head and poked dutifully at the vegetables Mrs. Marook pointed out. Kate caught Kirsten's eye and smiled. Kirsten responded by rolling her eyes. They moved on among the bustle of the market—men shouting their prices, pointing out their wares and food. A pair of American soldiers in full battle gear turned into the lane they were in, moving languidly, their assault rifles pointing down and chatting to each other in a broad southern drawl. They really did look foreign among the smaller, thickset, dark Iraqi people. Their blonde hair and fair skin stuck out a mile. Kate's eyes were drawn to a stand of bright gold bracelets, hundreds of them hanging from long poles, glinting in the sun shine. The man behind the display immediately came forward, noting her interest.

"I wonder how many of these are real gold," she said in a low tone to Rebecca and Declan. Rebecca smiled and said, "I'll find out." Declan yawned.

While Rebecca haggled with the merchantman in Arabic, Kate turned to Declan. "I'm sorry this is boring you to death," she said through a grin, "but it is very therapeutic for us . . ." Kate trailed off.

Declan looked down at Kate. She had lost her grin and had gone quite white.

"What's up Katie . . . you okay?"

Kate gripped his forearm with incredible force.

"What? Kate . . . What's wrong?"

He made as if to turn.

"Don't turn, just stay where you are."

Declan frowned down at Kate. Her eyes were riveted on something behind his left shoulder.

"What?" Declan intoned. His right hand slid down toward the holster under his tunic.

"No!" Kate whispered. Tears sprung from the corners of her eyes. Now Declan became alarmed. He felt the fierce grip again, keeping him in place in front of her. He frowned again and took Kate's hand off his forearm slowly, but firmly.

"Dekker, about five meters away and to the right . . . he's here. Dekker. Alive! There is a man with him; he has a gun in a holster," Kate whispered.

Declan froze. It took all his willpower not to turn around and have a look. He swallowed hard.

"The man behind him looks like a soldier," Kate said, still whispering and blinking back her tears.

"Oh God, please help us, they're coming this way."

Declan put his arm around Kate's shoulder and beckoned to her as if to look more closely at one of the bracelets.

As Dekker and the man in military fatigues with him walked past them, Rebecca, who had been negotiating with the stall owner and had missed the drama unfolding, turned and was about to speak when she noticed the white men standing over at the next stall. She looked at Katie and saw her stricken expression and had the presence of mind to speak in Arabic. Behind Kate, her beloved Dekker said in a very foreign-sounding English accent, "Tell this chap, I'll take a dozen of these oranges."

In front of them Lewis turned to see where the following group was and immediately saw Dekker, then Declan and Kate bent down as if examining the bracelets. The man with Dekker sensed a sudden rise in tension—perhaps the quietness that had descended on the people in the immediate vicinity of the

The Flame of Heaven

hubbub of the market. His hand dropped to his holster. Dekker noticed the movement and looked up.

"What's up Raphael?" he said.

Raphael did not answer, his eyes on someone ahead. Dekker turned and as he did so his hand brushed the bag of oranges he'd purchased moments ago. They tottered and rolled into the dust.

"Damn." Dekker ducked down and started to pick up the scattered fruit.

This brought Raphael's attention back to the present.

"You idiot!" Raphael said.

Dekker looked at him, annoyance written all over his face.

"Instead of being a completely useless ass, why don't you help me pick these up?" The oranges had rolled across the causeway and under the feet of a couple standing across from Dekker. The man turned and smiled and picked up two oranges to give them back to Dekker. Dekker thanked him. The woman with him stooped and picked up an orange. The man with her tried halfheartedly to take it away from her, but she insisted. She turned and looked at Dekker.

Dekker's knees almost gave way; he wobbled slightly. Kate's eyes, blue and beautiful and brimming with tears, looked back at him. The man with Kate took the orange gently from her hand. His eyes darted toward Raphael. Raphael had stooped to pick up an orange that had rolled the other way and so for a moment they were safe.

Declan whispered very low, so that Dekker caught only the faintest words: "She is safe, follow us."

Kate nodded once, slowly. The man turned and led Kate away.

Dekker's heart hammered in his chest. He bent down again and made as if to arrange the retrieved oranges in a more secure way in the plastic bag he carried.

"Okay, butter fingers, here is the last of the oranges," Raphael said. He dropped them into the proffered bag as Dekker rose.

Raphael caught Dekker's eye and knew there was something amiss. He searched the man's face in front of him, his hand brushing against the pistol butt again.

Raphael's eyes darted across after the departing group and then back to Dekker.

"What's wrong Dekker, you got ants in your pants?" he said.

"Just pay the chap, would you, and let's go."

Raphael searched his face again.

"Dekker, let me give you a friendly warning. Any crap from you and I'll plug you full of holes . . . you got me?"

Dekker held his eyes with a steely gaze. Raphael was first to blink; he turned slowly and paid the stall attendant—who had witnessed everything and stood with his gaze averted.

Dekker walked away to the next stall.

"Hey, slow down, cowboy," Raphael said sarcastically.

"What, are you going to shoot me in the back?" Dekker said and pushed on. He did not want to lose sight of the group ahead of him.

Chapter 37

Ali was good for his word. He introduced Shelomo and Marook to his uncle, the foreman Farzan Hassan. The older man had looked Shelomo and Marook up and down. "So you spik Engish," he said in broken English.

"Yes sir, we do," Shelomo said.

"And your friend?" asked Ali's uncle.

"I too speak English," Marook said.

"They can throw cement too, Uncle," Ali added in Arabic enthusiastically.

His uncle glared at him. "They are personal friends of yours?"

Ali swallowed. His uncle was a hard man.

"They are good men, Uncle, they gave me and my friends a lift from Baghdad."

Farzan made a kind of clicking noise in the back of his throat that spoke eloquently of impatience.

"Wait here. You, Ali and your friends go over to that tent and put your name down for work in the western sector."

"What about . . . ?"

"Go Ali! So help me God, or I will send you back to your mother!" That sent the youths scampering as fast as their thin legs could take them.

Uncle Farzan looked at Shelomo and Marook, "Your names?"

They told him.

"Where did you learn to speak English?" he said in Arabic.

"Overseas, sir. In England, we studied there when we were young men."

Farzan nodded. "Yes, in better days. None of our youngsters can speak that language any more."

Shelomo smiled, "Our country has gone through hard times."

The burly foreman grunted, then added, "We are getting a delegation of UN people with a special team of archaeologists later today from Baghdad. They have top priority. Praise be to Allah, you are a godsend. My worthless nephew has been helpful for a change. We need people to be able to interpret for us. These UN people are our financial backers, so I want no mistakes and God help you if you are lying to me about your abilities."

"Rest assured, we can speak English very well," Shelomo said with a smile, in English.

The foreman grunted again, "Follow me," he said, then called another young man over with a click of his fingers, "Mohamet, you register these others. I am taking these two to the UN tent."

"Yes sir."

Ali's uncle set off without a backward glance. Shelomo and Marook followed at a respectful distance.

"Clearly a man of authority," Shelomo said, and smiled. Marook grinned back.

"We have been very fortunate. We may yet meet our enemy face to face."

Chapter 38

The group ahead of Dekker moved leisurely, allowing him to do the shopping for fruit that he had been sent to do by Lord Ashworth when they had arrived in Baghdad. Dekker guessed that Lord Ashworth had sent him shopping in order to try to humble him, but it had worked out to be a blessing in so many ways, first, to get away from the oppressive presence of Lord Ashworth and Dupree, and the detestable presence in Professor Whitely. Dekker had contemplated violence on several occasions, once quite seriously while they were in the air over Baghdad, in a private Lear jet. It had occurred to him that if he could kill everyone on board by causing the plane to crash, then this whole conspiracy or tomfoolery or whatever this was, would be over with. He would never, of course, see Kate again. Dupree put an end to that. He seemed to be able to read Dekker's mind and had cuffed him to the seat he was in and brought him a bottle to pee into. Raphael had been instructed to hold up a blanket while he peed. The young lout guffawed rudely. Dekker had vowed to himself that he would get even, no matter what.

And now, now this golden opportunity had emerged; he had to move slowly and appear as normal as possible. Somehow Raphael had picked up on his excitement. Not to worry. He loaded the backpack with more fruit—pineapples with their spiky leaves cut off, dates, grapes, and grapefruit. That should do it.

The group ahead of him headed toward a set of low buildings to the far right of the bazaar.

"I've got to go," Dekker said evenly and headed toward the buildings.

"Hey . . . hey I didn't give you permission. Besides we have to be back soon. We leave for Babylon this afternoon."

Dekker flipped Raphael the bird as he walked with long strides to the outhouses.

Dekker felt a hard stinging jab to his lower left rib that drew the wind from his lungs. He fell to his knees.

"Listen to me, my fine English bastard, or you will get hurt. You will hold your pee in until we get home," Raphael breathed into his ear.

From his position on his knees, Dekker saw the men with Kate enter the men's toilet block. Dekker staggered to his feet again. A group of women were watching them from the other side of the causeway, whispering excitedly, their expressions alight with expectation. He knew Raphael could not afford a scene. Lord Ashworth had made it clear that they were to keep a low profile.

"I am going to go and take a leak, whether you like it or not."

Raphael glared at him.

"One fine day I'm going to put a bullet through you, Dekker. We know you have a traitor's heart and we know how to deal with traitors."

Dekker turned slowly and tramped toward the toilet block, fully expecting another stinging blow. He made it to the door without hindrance, but then felt Raphael push the barrel of his pistol into the small of his back.

"Any stupid moves and you are gone. Lord Ashworth believes your usefulness is fast coming to an end. Once that jabbering idiot gives us what we want, you will both be disposable, so if you want to live, make sure you don't become a nuisance."

Ignoring the gun barrel jammed into the small of his back, Dekker took the daypack from his back and put down the bags of fruit he was carrying outside the door. The stench from the darkened interior of the outhouse was overpowering.

"You coming in with me sweetheart, or will you look after the fruit like a good dog," said Dekker. For his cheek, Dekker received another hard punch to the ribs. He staggered forward into the gloom of the toilet block.

A modesty wall blocked the view of the street from the urinal and a row of toilets, with no doors, on the opposite side of the long room. Dekker made his way to the urinal in the semi-gloom of the building. Once his eyes adjusted to the gloom, he made out a man he did not recognize standing just behind the short wall and another man, the one who had been with Kate, squatting over one of the long drop toilets, his kaftan hoisted above his knees. There was another man at the urinal. An uncomfortable silence grew. The other man finished up and left in a hurry.

"Hurry up, Dekker," Raphael said from the door.

Dekker did not answer; he actually did need to go and felt a stabbing pain in his kidneys as he relieved himself.

"Dekker, come out now!"

"Up yours!" Dekker said loudly.

Dekker heard Raphael enter the outhouse and saw him come around the short wall, gun drawn.

The man standing behind the wall kicked at Raphael with a low powerful front on kick. His boot hit Raphael solidly in the side of his body as he moved past. Dekker ducked instinctively, expecting the pistol to go off and not knowing where the bullet might land, but the pistol spun from Raphael's grasp. He heard the young thug gasp. The attack would have come as a great shock in his temporarily blinded state.

Raphael cannoned sideways into the long drop stall on the other side of the room and right into the fist of the young man whom Dekker recognized. He fell to the earth like a sack of coal and knocked his head hard as he landed.

Dekker judged that he was fortunate it was not a cement floor. The young gunman lay still.

The man who had kicked Raphael produced a cord belt from under his kaftan. Without a word he unceremoniously flipped the unconscious man onto his stomach and tied his hands firmly behind his back. He then removed Raphael's shoes and stuffed one of the gunman's own socks into his slack-jawed mouth. He undid the laces of one boot and tied Raphael's ankles together. He did this so expertly, that Dekker started to wonder just who these men were.

"Dekker?" said the other young man, in a thick Scottish accent.

"Aah, yes?" Dekker said, trying not to sound nervous.

"Do up your zipper man. This is a godsend. I'm Declan, that's my brother Lewis trussing the turkey. The girls have gone to pick up the Land Rover. Kate is safe and well. You will see her soon. What we need to do right now is move this fella out of here as quick as we can and to our safe house where we can decide what to do. Okay?"

"Yes, sure. What do you want me to do?" Dekker said.

Lewis lifted his head and said, "There's an alley heading north just across the way. You take his shoulders, I'll take his legs and if anyone tries to stop us, Declan will deal with them. Once we're safe you tell us your story. We don't have any time to lose. Let's go!"

There was not time to ask questions or even think. Dekker hooked his hands under Raphael's armpits and they moved awkwardly into daylight.

Declan picked up the bags of fruit and the day pack. It seemed at first, as if no one would notice them; they made the alley, just about fifty meters distant, between two rows of mud brick houses, before Dekker heard the first signs of alarm. There was a sudden surge of interest; an arc of questioning faces turned their way.

"He is sick, our friend is sick, we are taking him home now," Declan said to the watching throng and nodded and smiled.

"Okay boys, on the double," he said, as he entered the alleyway.

A group of curious faces looked down the alley at them in wide-eyed astonishment. Dekker prayed fervently that no policemen or foot patrols would show up.

Up ahead was a Land Rover with the back tailgate thrown wide open, and standing to one side, the figure of a woman he would always remember, no matter how hidden behind clothing, her face a revelation of pure joy and tears. Sobs wracked her frame. The group of men burst from the alley and Dekker placed Raphael none too gently onto the tailgate and then turned to Kate who came running into his arms. He hugged her tightly to himself and felt her body shaking with all the pent-up emotion of the last three months. He held her face and looked into her shining eyes. The other women formed a small arc to their right. Behind them Lewis slammed the tailgate of the Land Rover closed.

"Okay lovebirds, let's get going, before the constabulary arrives," he said with a smile.

They all scrambled into the SUV, Dekker holding tightly to Kate's hand. He vowed to himself then that no one would separate them again, not ever.

Chapter 39

Shelomo turned from the section of wall that they were rebuilding. A buzz of excitement ran through the UN tent. They were close now and excavating the place where Shelomo remembered the Temple of Gula to be. He was sure they were at least digging on the right side of the ziggurat mound. This area had been excavated before in the late nineteenth century, but then without the aid of power tools and sophistication. The first archaeologists in Mesopotamia had been little more than adventurers and treasure hunters. Shelomo felt certain then and he still felt certain now that the orb had not been found.

He recognized Lord Ashworth instantly and looked for Dekker's lanky figure among the group. A dark man who carried himself smoothly walked beside Ashworth, speaking into his cell phone. *That was Dupree,* Shelomo thought. Next to him, an old man with wild unkempt hair. Something like an electric shock ran through Shelomo as he looked at the man. The old man's wild eyes searched the crowd of people before him; he looked agitated and was mouthing something to himself. Shelomo turned away slowly, not wanting to attract attention through sudden movement.

How was it possible? Could it really be? He felt himself shaking with fear. Kate had told him what had happened in the house, but there was a part of him, at least, that did not want to believe it was possible. *Well, it was possible; anything was possible if the Lord allowed it,* he reminded himself. A presence—he knew not how to describe it—a palpable sense of

The Flame of Heaven

evil and oppression accompanied the old man. Shelomo felt a sudden stab of terror in his heart, another ancient one . . . in his bones he knew that this meeting was inevitable, but now that it came to it, all his sense of confidence vanished.

He placed the brick and mortar he worked with into the section of wall he was repairing.

Diagonally across from him, Marook made eye contact. Shelomo nodded slowly.

"Shelomo! Hey, Shelomo!" the foreman shouted in Arabic.

"Come, bring your friend, we have a new section to excavate. You will give instructions to the men."

"Yes, sir," answered Shelomo and did his best to emulate the humble shuffle of the average worker in Iraq, a sort of skipping run with bent knees and head bowed, displaying speed with humility.

The agitation of the old man accompanying Lord Ashworth grew in Shelomo's presence, the muttering becoming a jabber.

"What on earth is eating him, Dupree? And where in hell's name is Dekker when we need him. Have you managed to locate them yet? I told you Dekker was a flight risk."

Dupree looked at his master with dead black eyes. "No sir, but my men have just reported to me that something odd—an altercation between some white men took place in the market square. Some women said they saw two men fighting and then one of them being carried off by a group of men and the other, Dekker, by the description, helping the other men carry a body."

Lord Ashworth flushed visibly at the news. Shelomo could see that if they had not been in company, Ashworth would have torn strips from Dupree.

"Dupree you assured me that all would be well and that Dekker would probably be more compliant if he had a bit of air. It looks like Dekker's friends may be in the city already . . . What in G . . ."

"Sir, all exits to the city are blocked, every patrol in Baghdad has been alerted to be on the lookout, and house to house inquiries are being made as we speak. They will not get away."

"I hope for your sake you are right. We really don't want this sort of attention . . . and shut that jabbering dolt up!"

Dupree took the older man's hand and shook it gently, then shook his head. Lord Ashworth turned back to the UN man in charge of the reconstruction effort in Babylon. "Look we have permits to dig here. Some evidence was uncovered a while back, tablets that spoke of a possible haul of temple material in this vicinity. We want to make sure that no looting takes place . . ."

"Yes sir we were alerted to your arrival. Rest assured we have experts enough to ensure that no heavy-handed and amateur archaeology will destroy anything of significance, sir."

"Yes, thank you Doctor Hammil. In the meantime we have our own experts. Dr Hammil, meet Professor Whitely." Doctor Hammil stretched out his hand. Professor Whitely looked at it and jabbered.

"Eh, he is a little eccentric, but an expert in the field of Assyriology," said Lord Ashworth.

"Most pleased to meet you, professor. Your reputation precedes you," said Doctor Hammil with a genuine smile.

"Why I should have recognized you. I attended a lecture or two of yours in New York when you toured there some years ago."

Whitely squawked and glared at an Arab workman who had been led to the group by another local with a foreman's hat on his head.

Lord Ashworth looked embarrassed; Doctor Hammil shocked.

"Ah, the plane ride has not agreed with him, Doctor. Now, if you please . . . our information is that the excavation is to the right side of the ziggurat, when facing north and about fifty meters diagonally across. The temple of . . . Gula."

"Ah yes! Very good information you have too. That is the site of the Temple of Gula."

"Really? And tell me, Doctor, has this temple been excavated yet? Have you found any artifacts?" Ashworth asked smoothly.

"Well . . . ah, yes and yes. It has been excavated, as it happens. We punched through into a corridor when we were digging for the ziggurat foundations."

"Punched through, you say? I hope no damage was done, Doctor."

The doctor squinted up at Lord Ashworth and pushed the glasses on the bridge of his nose more firmly onto his face.

"Sir, with all due respect, we are as careful as we can be."

"Mmmm. Show me if you please."

"Well, see the thing is, it's not safe, sir. This whole site is littered with caverns and unstable structures beneath the earth."

"Show me," Ashworth snarled.

"Ah, okay. Could I see those permits please?"

Ashworth flicked his hand and Dupree produced permits and his International Court police badge.

"I see, a policeman. What . . ."

"Smuggling . . . sir," Ashworth said, through a sneer.

Doctor Hammil blanched visibly.

"Well, our security is very tight. I don't understand. What has been smuggled? We've only just broken through . . ."

"Doctor, you have a lot of questions. No doubt all very good questions, but I would like to ask some of my own. So if you don't mind let's get going."

The doctor took a deep breath, eyed his guest with beady anger and turned on his heel.

"Very well, come this way, but don't say I didn't warn you. I'm not taking responsibility." He turned to the foreman and said, "We need some men and get the head of security here at once." Then he threw back his shoulders and marched in the direction of the ziggurat mound, not looking back.

Professor Whitely did not move but was pointing at the Arab workman and stuttering.

"Come on, Dupree; bring the old Jabberwocky along," growled Lord Ashworth. He turned his head and saw the professor pointing at one of the workmen.

"Doctor, stop! Who is this man?" Lord Ashworth pointed at Shelomo, who followed the doctor.

"A workman who is able to speak English and will be helping direct the men you will need for your work . . . we anticipated that you might need to, you know, have some help whatever it is you are doing."

"What we are doing, Doctor, is making sure very valuable artifacts are not stolen," Lord Ashworth snapped, then turned his attention to Shelomo, "What is your name, man?"

"Shelomo, sir."

Lord Ashworth looked from Shelomo to the doctor, then the professor.

Whitely glared at the workman.

The workman lowered his gaze humbly.

Lord Ashworth chuckled, "You seem to have upset our prof. somehow."

He looked from one to the other again, "Do join us; we will need someone to direct the workers."

"Yes, sir. I'm sorry for your friend's trouble, sir."

Ashworth looked at Shelomo quizzically, and then chuckled again.

"You have no idea how troubling my old friend has been. But he has been useful."

"Shall we?" said Doctor Hammil testily, then turned and walked without a backward glance toward the stone and sand mound that was once the proud ziggurat of Marduk.

Shelomo swallowed hard as he followed the men. Marook followed at a discreet distance. The foreman had left them to gather some workers with picks and shovels.

As they neared the ziggurat Shelomo could see a taped-off section with a bright yellow sign that read "No Entry" in Arabic and English. The pole had been pushed into hard soil next to a trench.

The men looked down into the trench and saw a dark gash in the soil at its far end. An opening six feet by five feet, filled with drifts of dirt.

"As you can see, very unstable," Doctor Hammil said.

Lord Ashworth turned to the professor and opened his hands and pulled a face, as if to ask "Now what?".

The professor surged forward and started to climb down the ladder into the trench.

"Professor! Please!" Doctor Hammil cried.

"Oh, do stop fretting Doctor, I will take full responsibility. Go and get some rope and lamps and Shelomo here can bring a shovel or two. Dupree see to it."

The foreman came back just then with six men and looked at Doctor Hammil.

"Lord Ashworth I must insist. This is most untoward. Why on earth would you want to go down there now?"

Lord Ashworth turned on the doctor with such a look of venom on his face that it stopped the other man short.

"Doctor, no more, please I have my reasons. We are collecting evidence. No more questions. Do as you are told, or you will be relieved of your duty. Is that clear to you?"

The dumpy doctor pushed nervously at the bridge of his nose again, his glasses flashing in the bright sunlight. He swallowed hard.

"You have not the authority to relieve me of my post. I'm in charge!"

"Inspector Dupree here is in charge of antiquities theft and a member of the United Nations police force. He has the authority. I'm a presiding judge and while my authority as a judge does not extend to the area of our removal it does extend to the area of ensuring that the sovereign nation of Iraq is not robbed blind of its antiquities by an occupying force. Are we clear?"

"Yes, sir." Doctor Hammil said quietly. "Farzan, Shelomo, get the men ready, we are going down."

Chapter 40

"For heaven's sake, be careful!" shouted Doctor Hammil over the rumble of rock and dust tumbling down the shaft.

Men shouted in Arabic from the darkness.

"The men say they can see a way down through the jumble of stone into a chamber," Shelomo shouted up from where he stood in the opening.

"Good work, Shelomo," Lord Ashworth said. His mouth flashed a smile, but Shelomo was not able to see his eyes from behind his dark glasses.

The work had been rapid. The men had descended to a floor bed under the surface of the soil. Now they placed stanchions to keep the roof from collapsing. They had managed to dig out rubble along an ancient passage toward the entrance of the temple. Directions flowed between the group at the top and the men below. Shelomo was certain now that whatever was inside Professor Whitely knew exactly where the Flame of Heaven was located. It could be only one person. Shelomo at first thought he should try to throw them off the scent, but realized as he worked with the men that it was only a matter of time; they would find the burner if it was still there after all these years.

Darkness fell; Doctor Hammil pleaded with Lord Ashworth to stop. He was sent packing, and the men were promised double their wages to work through the night. Some of the men refused, saying it was against the will of Allah, and deserted. Lord Ashworth had the good sense to let them go. He tripled the wage and the more desperate of the men stayed on. Halogen lamps were brought in and several more supporting beams propped up the earth above their heads. Three hours passed as they worked steadily. The men came out for a break.

Lord Ashworth heaped praise on them through Shelomo, who served as interpreter. While they sat outside in the cold desert night, drinking hot tea and eating hunks of bread and cheese, Lord Ashworth called to Shelomo.

"Where are you from Shelomo?" asked Lord Ashworth.

"Well originally from around these parts, sir," said Shelomo quietly.

"I see. And where did you learn to speak English?"

"In England, sir. I was educated there . . . many years ago now."

Ashworth smiled mirthlessly.

"What do you think it is about the professor and you?"

"Perhaps I remind him of someone he does not like. When a man lives a long time, his thoughts sometimes get confused," said Shelomo thoughtfully. He held Ashworth's eyes. Something changed in Ashworth's face ever so imperceptibly. His eyes seemed to grow hooded and dark in the half light.

"Yes, Shelomo, you have no idea how accurate that might be. You have a strange quietness about you. The mark of leadership, it is unmistakable. Like one used to giving commands and expecting obedience."

Shelomo gave Lord Ashworth a half smile, "You too seem to possess such a spirit."

"Ha, a good answer—still intriguing. You have done well. You seem to know a bit about archaeology?" said Ashworth.

"I am acquainted with old things, sir."

Ashworth stared at Shelomo.

"Mmmm, I see. Tell me Shelomo are you acquainted with any old legends about this site? Objects of power, perhaps?"

"There are many such legends. Objects from Babylon's pagan past are very popular among those devotees of the occult."

"Are you such a devotee?"

Shelomo did not answer the question; he simply stared at the ground.

"Well, have I finally pinned you down—a good Muslim, or no? You are very evasive."

"The power of such objects, Lord Ashworth, does not reside in the object itself. The power is twofold—the power behind the object and the power that the object has in the devotee's psychology. The object acts as a door through which the secret power is revealed, or acts upon the devotee. In many respects the object itself is immaterial except for psychological and uh . . . I suppose one could say, spiritual purposes."

The hooded expression returned to Ashworth's eyes.

"You are an interesting man, Shelomo," Ashworth purred.

Behind him Shelomo felt rather than heard someone move. He turned to see Dupree and the professor standing close by.

Shelomo looked into Ashworth's eyes questioningly.

"We are looking for a particular object," Ashworth began.

"That is obvious, sir."

"I see," said Ashworth again. "Not many men would be bold enough to call me obvious."

Shelomo remained silent, returning Ashworth's stare.

"I like your spirit, Shelomo. You are a bold one." The two men were locked in a silent wrestle of wills. Neither dropped their gaze.

"The object is about the size of a football, made of bronze. A burner. Our information is that it is down in the room in which you dig. It may take some time to remove all that debris, but that is what we are after. If you find it, you will be well rewarded. You and your men will not stop working until we have found it. Dupree here will be accompanying you down there, together with the professor. He will tell you where to dig."

Shelomo nodded. "I understand."

That mirthless smile flashed again, but did not quite make it to Ashworth's eyes.

"Do you, Shelomo? When we are done here, I think you and I should have a little chat. Now go."

Shelomo turned and stopped short. The professor stood before him blocking his way.

"I know who you are? Could it be, after all these years, we meet again? You were a spy in the court of the great King Ahab," said the professor in fluent Babylonian.

Shelomo understood every word, though he had not heard the long extinct language spoken so well for many years. He stared into the old eyes in front of him, full of fierce pride and hate. Dekker seemed to have made contact with the others, but they were in trouble and so was he, if he did not play his hand very carefully.

Shelomo stepped around the professor, shaking his head and made to walk off. The professor's arm shot out and clutched his forearm with considerable strength.

"You cannot fool me. You know what we are after. I will be watching you closely," said the wretched old man.

Shelomo broke his grip none too gently and looked into Dupree's dead eyes. He turned without a word. He could feel all three sets of eyes burning into his back as he called to the men.

"Come, we are near the end and there is good money for those who stay. We are looking for a round bronze object. If you find it, do not attempt to touch it. Call me immediately."

The men rose with sighs and coughs, and trudged back toward the ditch with their picks and spades.

Shelomo moved off with the men and as he did so spoke quietly in Arabic to Marook. "The old one seems to know. Leave now and say you need the toilet, then find the others and get them to safety." Behind him unnoticed, Dupree made eye contact with Ashworth. Ashworth nodded imperceptibly as the men passed before him and down into the belly of the earth. Marook made to leave.

"Hey, where are you going?" Lord Ashworth shouted.

"He needs the toilet," said Shelomo, turning around immediately and not waiting for orders.

Ashworth looked at Marook for a few seconds with hooded eyes, then smiled and said, "Go," waving with his hand imperiously.

To Dupree he said, "Keep an eye on the one called Shelomo. I don't want him slinking off after we find the object, or even if we are unable to locate it. He is to accompany us back to Baghdad."

༺ ༻ ༺ ༻ ༺ ༻

As Shelomo and the men worked, he prayed with all his might. A great bitterness pressed in upon him. After all these years of anxiety and waiting and hoping, it had come to this. Shelomo sighed heavily and wiped his brow, although it was cold down in the hole beneath the earth. He knew the orb would be found, he knew he would not be able to protect it from them and he knew with certainty that he was now a prisoner.

A shout up ahead alerted him that something unusual had been found. All day and night they had been finding artifacts, some quite beautiful. An excited buzz ran through the men, then another shout, 'Watch out!" in Arabic.

Shelomo pushed through the throng of men and there it was. One of the men prodded it with his spade while another made the Shiite sign to avert evil. It glowed balefully in the dark, a fierce copper red. A hand shoved him rudely aside and the wild face of professor Whitely surged past him, closely followed by Dupree with his pistol drawn.

"Stop! Hey you're mad!" one of the men shouted at Whitely, as he grabbed what appeared to them to be a red hot object. He lifted it above his head and gazed longingly into the fiery depths of the orb, then his eyes fell on Shelomo. A crazed smile lit the old face in the glow of the Flame of Heaven.

Printed in the United Kingdom
by Lightning Source UK Ltd.
134848UK00003B/85-93/P